A Little Color in His Life

by

Cheryl A. Cornell

A Little Color in His Life

Cover Art by *Angela Anderson*

The Wild Rose Press
PO Box 706
Adams Basin, NY 14410-0706
Visit us at www.thewildrosepress.com

Publishing History
First Champagne Rose Edition, 2008
Print ISBN 1-60154-419-7

Published in the United States of America

"You're stunning," he whispered when he reached her side.

"Thank you." They stood together, ignoring the other people around them until a waiter paused beside them, offering glasses of champagne from his tray, which she declined. Several messages had been passed without a single word being spoken. The intensity between them was almost palpable.

"Let's get you something to drink that won't give you a headache."

He led her to the bar in the corner, where she accepted a glass of sparkling water. A hand slapped him on the back, and he reluctantly turned away from her. "Mike, good to see you, thanks for coming. How's business?"

Vincent saw that Mike was eyeing Darien, and she looked uncomfortable but she didn't interfere in their conversation. Finally, when he had no choice, Vincent made the introduction.

"Mike, I'd like you to meet Darien West." Mike's leering look at her had Vincent positioning himself between them. The other man took his hint, but moved away a bit too slowly. Darien held back a smile, her bottom lip between her teeth.

Vincent leaned closer. "Don't bite your lip, let me." And he did, right there in front of all his guests. His mouth found hers, tugging her lip with his teeth before capturing her in a long-awaited kiss. When he pulled back, she kept his eye.

"An effective way of marking your territory," she whispered, her voice almost hesitant.

"I suppose you could view it as that. I saw it mainly as a chance to kiss you."

"Two things accomplished at once. No wonder you're such a productive business man! You multitask beautifully." She threw back her head, favoring him with one of her husky laughs.

Dedication

For Rich. Thank you for making my writing
a priority in our everyday life.

Thanks to family and friends who read, edited,
and gave honest opinions.

Thanks to everyone at The Wild Rose Press,
especially my editors,
Roseann Armstrong & Lili Booth.

Chapter One

She placed her bid with only the hint of a nod.

The auctioneer must know her well, Vincent decided, noting she didn't hold a wooden paddle with a number. From his vantage point in the private viewing room above, he'd watched her walk down the red-carpeted path with one of the senior appraisers. She took the reserved seat the appraiser indicated before presenting him with one amazing smile. Vincent stood and walked closer to the darkened window to get a better look. It didn't escape him that the older man walked with a slight bounce in his step after his encounter with the brunette. Although her back was to him, Vincent could see her erect posture and a long length of leg covered in nude silk from her knee to her foot, which was slipped into a pair of black, three-inch sling-back pumps.

His insides tingled in a way that they hadn't in a long time. Taking a step back, he retrieved the crystal glass he'd been drinking from. With a long sip of the amber liquid, he took in the rest of the package she presented.

Long sable hair fell past her shoulders in soft waves. The overhead lighting reflected both blonde and red highlights. She wore a silky-looking dress in ice green; it shimmered with every movement she made. The long sleeves were pushed back toward her elbows, and several diamond bracelets on her left wrist mingled with a bracelet watch.

He couldn't tell if she wore earrings because her hair covered her ears. He knew on first sight she was tall. The man in the seat next to her was a lawyer he'd been introduced to several times. He knew the man was at least six feet. This woman held her own beside him. She didn't look at the program in her hand, but instead settled in her seat and whispered to the man next to her.

Knowing of the lawyer's wife's jealousy, Vincent pulled back a smile as the two sat with their heads close, her hand coming up to shield their hushed words from those around them. He saw long fingers with red tips and well-shaped hands, her left ring finger unadorned. He also watched the lawyer's wife make her way toward them, the sight of her triggering their names, Sissy and Lyle Dawkins. Instinct made him watch the encounter and wait to see how the women reacted. He wasn't prepared for the lack of confrontation.

Instead, when the brunette was tapped on the shoulder, she slowly turned and, after a second glance, stood to envelop the lawyer's wife in a warm hug. He watched them kiss each cheek, actually touching lips to skin instead of kissing the air around them as so many women did in these false meetings. They didn't pull away afterwards, both women holding the embrace. He wished he knew what they were saying, for a moment later the brunette threw back her head and laughed openly. Only after the second hug did they release their hold on each other.

Lyle Dawkins stood and moved down a seat, allowing the two women to sit beside each other. Somehow Vincent was relieved and disappointed. None of it made sense. But the stirring continued inside him.

Vincent watched the auction with half an eye, waiting for his item's turn at the block. While he still hadn't gotten a full-face look, she intrigued him, and it had been a long time since a woman caught his eye. Maybe it was her posture, sitting instead of slumping, or the laugh she'd shared with Sissy Dawkins. Whatever it was, his assistant Mark had to clear his throat to get his attention. Only then did he pull himself out of his self-imposed stare and watch the proceedings below. Vincent took the cell phone handed to him and watched for Timothy's nod from the floor. Timothy stood to the side, a clipboard in hand, his headset in place, his young face serious. They passed a few pleasantries before the bidding began.

The item that brought him here tonight was up next. He wanted it and would get it no matter what the cost. At the preview earlier last week, he'd run his hand along the antique English oak, felt the texture worn smooth from years of use, and knew he wanted it for his new home. At least he'd seen its forty-foot length before the plans were final. He'd already spoken with the architect and the builder and had been assured that adding the extra footage needed to accommodate the piece wouldn't be a problem at this point in the design process. Now his interest in the item had become secondary to his interest in the woman in the green dress, who seemed to be friends with everyone she came in contact with. He let several bidders outbid each other and was pleasantly surprised when it was down to one telephone bidder and himself. His groan only came after the serious bidding started; he wasn't prepared for the third participant.

With only the slightest movement of her head, she upped his bid.

Vincent stood abruptly when he realized it was her bid. They managed after two rounds to lose the telephone bidder and now it was between him and her. God, he thought, he wanted to know her name. And he wanted to get the piece for himself even if that meant spoiling her fun. With a half-smile, he wondered what her reaction would be to losing it. He didn't have to wait long; two more rounds and she watched Timothy intently. After his last raise she turned to the private viewing rooms and searched the black glass. He took a step back even though he knew he couldn't be seen. Whatever it cost him would be worth it. The first look he got of her face, full on, would be burned into his memory for all his days. Her eyes were wide, the color all but obscured by the glass, and her cheeks slightly flushed. Scanning above, her look changed from curiosity to loathing in a flash. He laughed aloud as she slowly turned back in her seat, chin up, and clasped her hands in her lap.

Vincent waited until she upped his bid. He automatically upped hers. For one prolonged minute he waited to see what she would do. They had gone over the estimated price and he knew she was mentally calculating how much further she might go to win. Again, the slightest of nods and again he spoke into the phone. Timothy raised her. Two more turns and she took a deep breath. When the auctioneer asked her if she was through, she gave him a positive nod. Only then—-after the traditional, once, twice, sold to Timothy's telephone bidder did Vincent relax. He waited to see what she would do but it seemed nothing at the moment.

With a snap decision, he turned to Mark.

"Head downstairs and invite her up for a drink." The younger assistant moved quietly from the room, straightening his tie and tugging at his jacket.

He knew deep inside she wouldn't accept his offer, but he watched as Mark waited to the side for an opportunity to approach her. While he couldn't hear their conversation, he saw her take the offered business card and study it. He watched her read the information and then turn to look at the upper gallery, instantly knowing she'd been right in her assumption that the person who outbid her on the antique bar was behind the blackened glass. She handed the card back to Mark and shook her head, *No*. Vincent dragged in a breath of air and held it as Mark made the offer a second time.

And for a second time she said no.

Mark looked to the gallery and slowly moved away. Vincent noticed Sissy Dawkins speaking to the woman, only to be dismissed with a shake of her head. With the short break over, she settled back in her seat, not offering Sissy any information on the invitation as she animatedly spoke a second time, looking up to the dark gallery.

Mark had returned in a state of dismay. "I'm sorry, Vincent. She said she wasn't interested. I tried rewording your invitation, but she still said no."

Vincent dismissed it easily. "You win some and lose some. The important thing is I now own the bar, and it's going to look great in the den of the new house, all forty feet of well-worn, two-hundred-year-old oak."

Mark seemed relieved but confused.

In all the time he'd been working for Vincent Leighton, Mark had never seen him walk away from any encounter until he'd won. While not letting on to Mark that he too was surprised, Vincent continued to watch her, wondering just who she was. A rare woman indeed. Most men and women would have kept the card as a souvenir.

Mark reminded him of a business deal last year.

"Right, the electronics firm I purchased," he mumbled, more to himself than to Mark. Vincent remembered their meetings, the party where he met Sissy, and the brunch he'd attended with them. He also remembered the numerous invitations he'd refused Sissy. Hopefully, if push came to shove, she would be the opening he might need later.

The brunette intrigued him and that was rare. Most women he'd met in the last ten years didn't interest him. Some assumed he would be their knight and rescue them. They were usually prissy and beyond needy. Or they went overboard in the other direction, assuming male roles and wielding power with an eye toward vengeance, just waiting for a man to make one small misstep that they could pounce on. Vincent didn't waste his time with either type.

What intrigued him was a woman who stood up for herself and her opinions, whether it was the popular consensus or not. And, most of all, this dark-haired beauty was tall and lean. She'd reminded him of Kim Novak in those movies from the 1950s. Her image had been burned into his sixteen-year-old brain the first time he saw an old movie of hers. Tall and slim, her curves in all the right places. This woman had a buxom, hourglass figure to be proud of, and her slim waist flared into wider hips. Her belly was flat and her legs long.

Vincent pulled the tie from his neck, dropping it in his suit pocket, and opened the top two buttons of his shirt as he left the private area, slipping into the back of the auction room just before the event ended. There he waited until he saw her heading toward the exit. Timing his approach carefully, he stalled and was able to hesitate to let her go through the door first. In the process he caught her eye.

He hadn't expected to be overpowered by her spicy scent and he hadn't counted on her eyes being the lightest green he'd ever seen. The dress she wore matched them exactly. His mouth had gone dry and his lips dropped open slightly. He was instantly annoyed. He had to swallow the lump forming in his throat when she offered him a smile for his polite gesture. Vincent only nodded his head as she walked before him, using the opportunity to watch her walk away. He stopped dead in his tracks to give her some distance and moved only after a man behind him cleared his throat to get his attention, both men taking in the sight of her long legs as they moved away on swaying hips.

Outside in the cooling fall night, he took a direct path toward Sissy Dawkins. She smiled before he reached her, her hand extending out toward him. He knew the public acknowledgement would suit her as well as his own purposes. His embrace was light and she all but bubbled around him, tugging on Lyle's arm to get his attention. After several minutes of forced pleasantries, he spotted his green-eyed beauty. Following his glance, Sissy called out loudly, "Darien, over here, darling," forcing her to turn toward him.

So, her name was Darien. It fit her.

He watched several emotions pass over her classic features, first annoyance, then dread, and finally acceptance. Her long legs covered the distance quickly and she was before him once again. Bangle bracelets on Sissy's arm rattled when she reached to Darien.

"Darien, I'd like you to meet Vincent Leighton. Vincent, this is Darien West."

They nodded toward each other and waited while Sissy told him Darien was a designer. She'd apparently done wonders with their new apartment. It was the opening he needed and he took it.

"Really, that's wonderful. I've been looking for someone to give me a few ideas on a place I'm working on out east." Her green eyes flashed gold around the rims when she was angry, he realized. Even in the low outside light, he saw the change.

"Oh, then you simply must let Darien take a look. Why, before she worked her magic I wasn't sure I'd be able to make a home out of our place, but in she walked and it all turned out wonderfully. You must come to Sunday brunch and take a look, Vincent."

Sissy looked as though she was holding her breath waiting for his answer, knowing if Vincent Leighton did accept her invitation, her social calendar would be full for a year.

He shook himself. "I'd like that. I'll have Mark call you during the week and see if we can put something together in the next few weeks." Sissy continued to bubble over and Lyle had the good sense to tune her out.

Darien, on the other hand, kept her eyes fixed on Vincent, her attitude apparent. She wasn't happy at his second attempt to meet her. The Dawkins car arrived and Lyle asked Darien if she wanted a lift. Another perfect opening and Vincent took it.

"I was about to ask Ms. West if she'd like a drink. Maybe she'll tell me about your project. If she's interested, I could give her a brief idea of what I'm building."

From the look on Sissy's face, it was a done deal. There was no room to wiggle out of the situation gracefully, so Darien accepted his offer. Vincent expelled the breath he'd been holding while waiting for her answer as Lyle dragged Sissy away. Her last words as she was being seated in the car were, "Remember to have Mark call me." Finally assured it would happen, Sissy allowed herself to settle in the backseat of their car. Once the vehicle doors were closed, Vincent looked at Darien head-on. He nodded to the side of the crowd, guiding her by her elbow toward the fringes.

"I know it was an underhanded way to get you to have a drink with me. Are you mad?" It would be best to find out what he was dealing with right from the start. Her throwing her head back and laughing openly wasn't an option he'd thought of.

"It seems, Mr. Leighton, that I really don't have

much of a choice." Her voice was low and smooth, just short of husky. The smile she treated him to was similar to the one she'd favored the appraiser with and he knew he'd walk with a slight bounce in his step.

"A means to an end, Ms. West."

She watched him closely before speaking. "Do you really have a project, or was that part of your line too?"

Vincent laughed outright with her and placed his right hand over his heart. "Ms. West, you crush me. Would I lie about a thing like that, especially when it's a detail that could be checked so easily?"

"I don't know, Mr. Leighton. Would you?" She held his eye confidently.

"No. But I would like a chance to spend some time with you." He decided right then that the best way to handle a woman like Darien was with the truth.

"Why?" She stood her ground, becoming even taller, if that was possible. Standing next to his six-foot-four body, she was almost eye level with him, waiting for his answer. The longer she waited, the more her lips curled into a smile.

"Because you're tall." He hoped the frank answer would further his cause.

"Anything else?" She was baiting him. They both knew it. Vincent decided he liked her approach to the situation and would play along.

"You're not hard to look at, and I have it on good authority that you can do wonders with the worst of jobs. After all, it seems you survived Sissy and Lyle's project. That in itself should go down in the history books as a bonus for you." He flashed her his best smile and tried to remember the last time he had to work so hard to get a woman's attention.

"And?" She was still daring him. He liked her directness.

9

"And it will be a whole lot easier to kiss you goodnight when there aren't so many people around us." He hesitated only a second before adding, "Unless you want an audience..." Her cheeks flamed and he fell in love with her, then and there, standing on the sidewalk outside the auction house.

"I'll skip the audience and the kiss, but I'll accept the drink on those terms. Besides, since you can afford the bar you bought tonight, I don't think one drink will bankrupt you." His hand came up and moments later a town car pulled to the curb beside them. He held the door and didn't turn away as she folded her legs into the luxury interior. The driver pulled away after Vincent told him the name of a blues club that would be their destination. They didn't talk or make any pretense to try to. Instead, they sat quietly beside each other until the driver pulled up before the chosen destination.

The club was dark and smoky, a rarity for a public place in this day, while the music was sultry. The restaurant had changed into a private club after the no-smoking bans in restaurants started. While Vincent wasn't a heavy smoker, other than an occasional cigar, he enjoyed the atmosphere of the place as well as the style of music they offered. The yearly dues were insignificant when compared to the enjoyment he got from the time he spent there. They were greeted and seated immediately. Darien ordered decaf coffee and Vincent seconded her order. With a sly smile, he finally broke their silence.

"Are you afraid you'd lose your head and let me kiss you good night if you had a drink?" He'd meant to tease her, but it somehow came out more of a challenge.

"No, I rarely drink." There was no apology in her tone.

"Is that because you lose your inhibitions and become a wanton woman?"

"Only in your dreams, Mr. Leighton. Actually, I'm hypoglycemic. That's the reverse of a diabetic, and alcohol in my system doesn't process as it might in yours. It generally gives me a headache."

"I see. So you're a cheap date." She threw back her head and laughed aloud.

"No, never that," she all but whispered, holding his look to punctuate her words.

"I didn't think so." He waited while the waiter left their coffee. He saw she took it black with one sugar, real sugar. "But you put sugar in your coffee?"

"A little. It's generally the combination of sugar and starch in the alcohol that doesn't agree with me. If I'm careful, I can enjoy sweets, just in moderation."

"That explains your figure." Vincent wished he'd kept the thought to himself, but it was too late to retract it.

For a deafening minute, she sized him up, and finally laughed. "Relax, Mr. Leighton. I'll accept that as a compliment. Although my trainer would be crushed to hear it."

"How about we start with you calling me Vincent?"

"I suppose that could be arranged, but then you'd want to call me Darien and I'm not sure I'm comfortable with that just yet." She winked at him before bringing the cup to her lips.

"I'm not making any points here, am I?"

"No, not yet," she answered easily. "Out of practice, or was I supposed to swoon at your earlier invitation?"

He liked her easy ability to tease him. "I just wanted to apologize for outbidding you on the bar." He gave her his best puppy-dog look and knew it wasn't helping. She was holding back a laugh by biting on her lower lip.

"Oh, a nice guy, huh? Well then, how about

letting me buy the bar from you?"

"I'm a nice guy but not a crazy one. You have no idea how long I've looked for a bar like that."

"Trust me, I can imagine." She didn't elaborate and he was disappointed.

"Where were you going to use it?"

"I'm working on a restaurant in Soho. It would have been perfect."

"Sorry, it's going in the den of my new home."

"That's got to be some home to house a forty-foot bar."

"It will be once it's finished. Right now it's more of a shell. There was a fire a few years ago and it was left in ruins. Only the front fieldstone wall and several of the fireplaces were structurally sound enough to work around." He watched as Darien sat back in her seat and carefully placed her cup on the saucer in front of her.

She stared in disbelief. "Please tell me you didn't buy the old Millner estate near Glen Cove?" Even the darkness didn't hide the fact she'd lost all color in her face. For the first time since he'd seen her earlier, she twisted her hands in her lap and her teeth took a small bite of her bottom lip between them. Her whole persona changed from one of confidence to sorrow.

"Yes, you're familiar with it?"

"Yes." She stood and picked up her purse. "Thank you for the coffee, and good luck with your home, Mr. Leighton. I must be going." She moved quickly but smoothly through the crowd. He managed to meet her at the door after throwing some bills on the table. She pushed through into the cool night air with him steps behind her.

"Darien, what did I say?" She halted but didn't turn around. Her hesitation allowed him the time to catch up with her, his hands going to her shoulders to turn her to him. "What is it?"

"It's nothing, Vincent. Good luck with the house. Please don't be offended, but I won't be able to help you with the project." She didn't look him in the eye; rather, she glanced at his hands on her shoulders.

He realized he was holding her and she didn't like it. He also knew once he let her go he'd never see her again. Vincent drew one long, deep breath and lowered his head. When his lips grazed hers, he felt the swift intake of her breath and exerted more pressure.

Her right hand came up to his chest, at first to push him away, but she didn't. Instead, she gathered the lapels of his jacket between her fingers and let him have his kiss. His tongue gently swept along her lips, tasting her. He seemed content to sample her. Only after she relaxed against him did he press his tongue between her lips. His exploration wasn't timid, yet it wasn't overbearing. It was a quest he'd undertaken and she seemed to understand he wouldn't be stopped until he was satisfied. It didn't help that her sigh urged him on. When she finally started to participate in the kiss, he felt his heartbeat quicken under her hand. Suddenly, she was kissing him instead of the other way around.

It was Vincent who finally pulled back to look at her. He waited to see her eyes and then went back for a second taste. Only then did she pull away from him, watching him intently.

"I'm not sorry; I've wanted to kiss you since I watched you walk into the room tonight."

"I'm not either. But this is where it ends. Good-bye, Mr. Leighton." She turned to walk away, but he called after her.

"Wait, I'll drive you home," he said, hoping to keep her with him a little longer.

"No, thank you." He watched her walk confidently to the corner, hail a taxi, and slide into the back seat before he signaled his driver.

"What the hell was that all about?" he said aloud to the empty sidewalk.

****

Vincent sat behind the massive slab of mahogany and sorted through the work that had piled up since he'd taken a mental break two days before. He'd gone to the office both days but found he was staring out the window, his workload untouched. After spending most of the first afternoon gathering information about her, he was still confused. His research told him she was just thirty and unmarried. Her list of clients read like a page in the *Who's Who* directory. The list of restaurants she'd designed was impressive. The information was only lacking in one area: her private life. Other than being single, there was little about her. Her degrees in architecture and engineering impressed him but gave him no insight into her personality. If only she hadn't looked at him with such dread when he mentioned the North Shore house.

On impulse, he phoned down to have his vehicle pulled around. He changed into jeans and a work-shirt and dropped the bomb on Mark's ears that he'd be gone for the day. Mark was obviously confused by the turn of events, asking if several projects had been completed. Vincent grumbled under his breath that he'd get to them, and left. Only after he was belted into the SUV and was entering the midtown tunnel did he let himself relax. Emerging back into daylight, he pushed a few buttons on the hands-free telephone and returned calls, keeping his mind busy for the length of the drive. One of them had been to Mark to set up lunch with Sissy Dawkins. The drive calmed him and he found himself wandering the work site that would one day be his home.

The front stone wall stood straight and proud, even though the original wooden door was long gone.

Through the archway he saw nothing but dirt and scrub growing up from the ground that would someday be his living and dining rooms. The back of the site was delineated by a stone fireplace. It too was scorched but waiting for a new life. Vincent walked around the site several times before going back to his truck. Seated behind the steering wheel, he let his mind imagine what it would someday look like. He only turned on the vehicle when the night air chilled him.

The drive back to Manhattan was delayed when he detoured to a restaurant that was on Darien West's referral list. He decided the innocuous white block building was hiding something fabulous inside, because from the outside it was nothing more than a white monstrosity. He gave the valet his keys and with a deep breath, entered into wonderland.

He wasn't sure what to expect from the exterior, but what he saw he never could have imagined. Like something out of the Arabian Nights, color and texture took center stage. The menu slated the food as all-American, steaks and chops. The atmosphere led him to relax and enjoy the electric feel around him. He ordered a drink at the bar and was pleasantly surprised when the bartender paused to talk with him.

"First time here?" he asked, placing the drink in front of Vincent.

"Yes, a friend recommended it."

"You won't be disappointed. The food's always excellent."

"I wasn't prepared to be taken back to Aladdin and his harem nights," Vincent answered, sipping the neat scotch.

"It's a trip all right. The chef had one idea, his partner another. From what I hear it almost came to blows until they found a designer they both liked. This was the end result. Different, to say the least."

"Definitely different. I can't say I don't like it, but it is different. Definitely colorful."

"Exactly what all three were going for."

"Then they managed it." Both men laughed.

"Let me know if you need anything. Your table should be ready soon."

Armed with that information, Vincent took his place and scanned the menu. His waiter was friendly but formal. The food was excellent. His eyes scanned the colorful room and he laughed to himself. Definitely not what he'd pictured in his mind, that was for sure.

His drive back to the city on a full stomach relaxed him. He went to the office and managed to clear his desk. At least Mark would be off his back tomorrow.

At home, he wandered each room of the apartment, trying to see it with a different eye. It had been designed and furnished when he saw it. The turnkey approach had worked for him at the time. All he had done was move in his clothes. The kitchen had needed a bit of attention and it had almost killed him to make those decisions.

Now, with the project on the island getting ready to start, he wondered if his plans were right. He'd originally had the house designed as he thought it was supposed to be. Now he wondered if he wasn't doing it to impress. Surely not himself. Then who? The business associates who would be entertained there? He had no significant other to conspire with, so besides himself, who was he pleasing with the design? The question weighed heavily on his mind. At the desk in his study, he pulled a legal pad from a bottom drawer, and then sharpened a pencil until it was pin-tipped. His hand flew over the paper; the end result was still the same. For years he'd had a house plan on his mind. When he found the sight, he let the architect work from the basics to what they were planning. Now it seemed more the architect's plan than his.

Vincent tossed the pencil on the paper in disgust. Even for him it was a lot of money and time to spend on a structure you weren't in love with, or at least in awe of. Somehow, his rambling arts-and-craft style design had turned high tech, with the original stone walls and fireplaces the only thing to link it with its history. He knew he wanted more from the house. What he was planning on building was just that: a house. He'd always envisioned it being a home. When he checked his watch, he saw it was just after ten. He dialed the architect's office number, knowing he'd get Stan Woolard's voice mail. He hung up after leaving a brief message; he figured Stan would be in a huge snit tomorrow morning by the time he called Vincent back. He didn't care; after all, it was his home and his money that was going to build the project. He should be the one to feel comfortable there, and today as he'd walked the site, he realized what was planned wouldn't suit him at all.

Chapter Two

Darien tossed aside the printouts she'd been scanning. After a long day with the owner of the Soho restaurant, they'd come to terms on a second design choice for the bar. She bit her bottom lip, remembering Vincent Leighton.

She'd sat quietly beside the stranger she'd only seen pictures of and heard stories about. He was as tall as she'd been told but much more handsome than his picture had led her to believe. His wasn't a perfect face; in fact, his imperfections made him human. The ridge on the bridge of his nose told her he wasn't afraid of physical contact. His jaw was almost too long, but his wide mouth and lips evened it out. He had a small crescent-shaped scar above his left eye and she'd wondered if it was from the recoil of a rifle. Her mind went into overdrive trying to remember what she'd read about him. Self-made millionaire by the time he was thirty, never married. The rest was a blur, and she'd silently berated herself for not retaining the rest of the information. At the time it had seemed frivolous, but now... Her take-out supper still sat on the kitchen counter, congealing in white cardboard containers. She'd made a pot of tea, and then switched to Diet Pepsi. She'd read all she could find on Vincent, which wasn't much. Oh, there was plenty about his business accomplishments, but little about his younger days and family life.

She was still pissed about losing the bar to him, and even more annoyed at his kiss. Actually, when she let herself really think about it, she was mad at herself for taking it to a second level. She had to acknowledge she had escalated the situation. Her hand had risen to push him away, but she couldn't, didn't. Instead, she'd let him capture her lips under his and knew she'd pulled him closer. Warmth ran through her.

She hated the idea she was attracted to him. Especially after realizing who he was. It was bad enough he was Vincent Leighton, but to find out he'd been the one to buy the Millner property from under her was too much.

While she wanted bile to churn and feed her anger, all she got was a remembered tingling on her lips. She decided she was losing her mind and stripped on the way to the shower. She knew she had finally gone over the edge as she cleansed her body, the image of Vincent holding her prominent in her mind. The soft cloth she was using stayed in one place a little too long, finally giving her the release she'd found elusive. Shocked yet sated by her actions, she pulled on her favorite old flannel bathrobe and headed to the kitchen to microwave her supper.

She hadn't expected the phone to ring after ten. At first she thought to let the machine get it but decided at this hour it might be important. Darien managed to hold back a groan when she recognized Sissy's voice on the other end.

"I know it's late, but I wanted to let you know brunch is all set for this Sunday. Vincent will be there and you simply must come and tell him how you worked wonders with this stuffy old place."

Darien's mind went blank and she heard herself saying, "All right; brunch sounds great." She hung up and tossed the receiver on the sofa with disgust. She should have said no. But she hadn't. At first she thought to call tomorrow and beg off, knowing she wouldn't. The microwave beeped and she pulled the hot plate out. Standing at her kitchen counter, she picked at the food.

She knew the heavy feeling she was experiencing was because of seeing him again. She tossed the fork in the sink, dropped the full plate next to it, and then ran water over the food to push it down the disposal. When the sink had cleared, she put the dishes in the washer and headed to the freezer. Her hand reached automatically to the far left corner where she always stuck the box of Creamsicle pops. Drawing one out, she felt instantly better.

****

Food was the last thing Darien wanted at eleven o'clock the following Sunday. She'd arrived on time, dressed in a grey flannel pantsuit. An emerald green silk shirt accented the paisley scarf tied around her neck. The decision to leave her hair down had not been an easy one. Earlier she'd all but thrown up her hands in defeat trying to decide what to do with it when it struck her she was dressing for Vincent. The realization was both horrifying and thrilling.

Sissy was her bubbly self and Darien was instantly thankful the job was complete. She could accept her in small doses, but the six months she'd worked with her had all but snapped the few nerves she had left. Across the room, Vincent seemed at ease in worn denim and a navy blazer. The lighter blue shirt under it enhanced his face and skin tone. And it was a damned handsome face at that. With a moment alone, she moved to the terrace and enjoyed the fall sunshine. She knew it would be him joining her as soon as the door opened.

"This high up, the air is so much cleaner," he said

"Mr. Leighton," she acknowledged, suddenly at a loss for words.

"I thought we were working with Darien and

Vincent?" She didn't answer or turn to look at him. Instead he joined her at the railing. "Are you really annoyed with me?" His voice was just past a whisper even though they were alone.

"I haven't decided yet. I've been debating all week." Finally she turned to look at him and knew it was a bad idea. His dark brown eyes were watching her intently. "Although this brunch isn't making you any points," she finished with a laugh.

"If I had approached you any other way, what would your response have been?"

"I don't know. I suppose it would have depended on the approach." One of his eyebrows shot up at the challenge.

"I had supper at Delano's this week. It's quite an interesting place." He seemed surprised at the laugh he got in response to his words.

"Interesting, you say. How was the food?"

"Wonderful actually, but the atmosphere wasn't the usual restaurant casual."

She laughed again. "Not restaurant casual. That's a new term for the place, Mr. Leighton. But I like it and it does seem to fit." She liked his smile, she liked that there were a few stray grey hairs at his temples. And she liked the way he was looking at her, as if she was something special. The thought made her pull back, but his soothing voice made her stay.

"What gave you the idea for the concept?"

Darien moved back to the railing and glanced at the traffic below. "I suppose it was conflict."

"Conflict?" he whispered back.

"Actually, yes. I was dealing with a small war, or battle if you like, between the owners. Both had very definite ideas on what they wanted and they were very far apart. One afternoon I was listening to them argue and I started sketching. I let my mind wander and before I realized it, they were both staring over my shoulder. It was the first quiet moment I'd had with those two." She laughed.

"They took one look and were a united front. It was so far from either of their ideas that it worked for them both. I'll never understand why I was thinking about Aladdin at that particular time. Maybe it started with the lamps. And awful lamps at that! Instead, we created a mock medieval pavilion in bold colors. All quite an adventure at the time."

"What would have been your second idea for the place?"

"Don't go there, please. I spent the first few weeks trying to figure out how we could meld King Arthur's knights in armor with baroque mirrors and Italian gilt. Not a combination I could visualize, and when I did, it horrified me. It kept bringing me back to warring parties and from there it was easy to trade King Arthur for Aladdin."

"Then you purposely left the outside blank?"

She nodded. "With so much going on inside, we all decided minimalist worked for outside. What did you like about it?" It bothered her that his opinion was important.

He hesitated before answering. "The chairs. Not so much the chair itself for its style, just that it was large enough to be comfortable, even for me."

"Unfortunately we both know this world revolves around the masses, and not many of us are close to six foot tall—," she scanned his body from head to toe,—"or over."

"You're right. It's not often I meet a woman I don't have to slouch down to kiss." His left hand moved close to her face, his thumb running under her eye. He stroked her carefully, then pulled his hand back, a single eyelash all but floating on the pad of his finger. "Make a wish."

Darien knew she turned several shades of red at his touch and another, deeper shade at his words.

Sissy interrupted them at that precise moment, asking them to come inside and join the rest of her guests for brunch. She didn't let Darien get past her without a wink.

It made Darien's stomach roll to think Sissy would now be forever telling anyone who would listen that she'd matched her with Vincent.

****

Darien tried to make an early escape but kept being stalled. First by Vincent, then Sissy. When she finally made it to the elevator her stomach ached and her neck was knotted. She closed her eyes and rotated her head several times in small circles. It was the strong hand placed on her neck from behind that put her in a defensive stance. Instinct had her elbow jamming back toward the offender. It wasn't until she heard his gasp that she realized what she'd done. In one smooth stroke she'd elbowed Vincent squarely yet firmly in the stomach. His hand dropped from her neck as he took a step back.

"Oh, God. I'm so sorry, Vincent...I didn't realize; I didn't think." His hand held his midsection while he measured his breathing. "Vincent, are you all right?"

When he finally lifted his head toward her, he saw the look of concern. His lips spread into a wide smile.

Darien breathed again and tried to think of what to say. "I'm sorry; I didn't realize you were behind me. I thought I was alone and then..."

"Yes, I get it, but who taught you that move?" His smile made her relax and she found it hard to hold back her own. It widened while he watched her try to bite it back, her teeth crushing her bottom lip to control the laugh threatening to rush forward. Instead of waiting for an answer he moved his hand to the back of her neck, pulling her head toward him. "Don't bite your lip, Darien, let me..." His words didn't register, but his actions did. His lips covered hers as his teeth pulled at her bottom lip and sucked it into his mouth. The tip of his tongue slid over it several times before she relaxed against the wall of his chest and surrendered to his kiss.

The arrival of the elevator quickly broke them apart. The cab was empty, and she pushed the lobby button more times than needed. Vincent stood several feet away from her, his hands clasped in front of him.

"Does the elevator have video and sound or just video?"

"Just video that I'm aware of," she answered automatically.

"Good. My truck is parked just outside, come with me for a ride. I'd like to show you something."

"I don't think that would be a good idea, Mr....Vincent." She didn't turn to him, instead became very interested in the descending numbers above the door. "I suppose after that kiss, calling you Mr. Leighton is ridiculous."

"Come with me, Darien. It's a beautiful Sunday afternoon for a ride. I'll have you back before dark, if that's what you still want."

She couldn't believe his gall. "I think not, Vincent. Somehow I don't think..."

"Don't think, Darien. Just this once, don't think, please?"

"Where?"

"For a ride, and I'm a very good driver."

"And you'll have me home before dark?"

"If that's what you want, yes. Just give us a few hours to..." The elevator doors opened onto the lobby and their conversation was stalled. He guided her by her elbow around the waiting people, toward the door. Outside in the sunshine and fresh air, he directed her to the side. "Well?"

"I somehow feel that even if I said no, I'd still

wind up in your car." She stared at him, trying to decide what to do. "I don't really know you."

"We can rectify that, and no matter what, I'd never hurt you in any way."

"That's what they all say."

"I'm not all or everybody. In fact, I'm as far away from the norm as you could find. And so are you. That's part of what attracts me to you." He held back a smile but not very well.

"Besides that I'm tall?" she teased.

"There's that too." He moved closer, entering her personal space. His words moved a few hairs near her ear just before his hand reached up and traced her chin. He settled with his fingers on her neck, his thumb near her lips. Automatically, her tongue reached out to moisten them and his finger followed its path.

"Vincent, I'm not in the market for an affair."

"Neither am I, Darien. Neither am I," he whispered as he closed his mouth over hers. When he finally leaned back, there was no question that she would leave him. He motioned for her to turn right and his arm went to her waist, tugging her closer. He only released her when he opened the vehicle door.

"I'm not sure this is a good idea, Vincent. In fact, I think it's really bad, one we shouldn't let happen." Her words assaulted him as soon as he opened the driver's door. Settling behind the wheel, he turned to study her.

"Are you afraid of me or all men?" His tone was serious—too serious, she realized.

"*No.*"

"Answer me, Darien."

"Not all men, just you." Her eyes flashed from emerald to gold.

"Good, I like a woman who knows when to be afraid. But there are levels of afraid, and I'd never hurt you willingly."

"I'm not looking for..."

"Neither was I," he whispered as he turned the engine on. "Do I drive you home or...?" He turned down the radio and glanced at her.

"Or?"

"Tell me what you want, Darien."

"Where are you taking me?" She wasn't sure where the words had come from, but looking at him she didn't want to let it end. As soon as she asked, he smiled at her and then turned to pull out into traffic.

"I hate smug men, Vincent." Darien crossed her arms over her chest and turned to look out the side window.

"Not smug, Darien. Just confident."

"Sometimes the two meet and get confused."

"Sometimes, but not today. It's my day off and I want to go for a drive with a beautiful woman beside me. What's wrong with that?" She refused to acknowledge the taunt in his voice.

"At the moment I don't know, but I'm sure by the time this day is over we'll both have several opinions." His hearty laugh wasn't what she expected, and her joining him wasn't what she'd imagined. Whenever she was around him, her responses took on a life of their own. Just the fact she was sitting beside him in his truck on her way to who knew where was beyond out of character. He seemed to understand and waited until they were inside the tunnel before speaking.

"You don't like that I'm in control, do you?"

"No. Not at all. And I can save you the trouble of the rest of your drive. You can take the first exit after the tunnel. I don't want to go to Millner's." Darien cursed herself. She should have known this was where he'd take her. Accepting that she'd subconsciously wanted to come back to the old place was difficult on many levels.

****

That was exactly where they wound up, parked beside the nonexistent home that once graced the acreage around them. When he turned off the ignition, he released his seat belt, but didn't move from the vehicle. Vincent leaned back and waited her out. Only when she let out a heavy breath did he speak.

"Why do you hate it?"

His simple words made her heart ache and she knew she would tell him the truth. All the way out she'd thought to give him a line about it. She would say she didn't like the lot or the area or whatever she could come up with. Instead, with five simple words he'd shown his hand; he'd let her know this land meant something to him.

Sighing, she turned around to look at him. "I don't hate it. I never have." With those words she let herself out of the truck and wandered slowly toward the front wall.

He followed her a few paces back. She knew he was watching her as she took in the sight, realizing she had some connection to the place.

"I don't understand. Why did you leave the bar the other night after I mentioned it, and why fight me to come here? None of it makes any sense."

Vincent continued to watch as she bent to pick up a charred fragment of wood, turning it over in her hands several times. The charcoal stained her fingers, but she didn't care, using her nail to scrape away some of the black.

"Darien, I'd really like to know. I understand it doesn't make any sense since we hardly know each other, but your opinion means something to me."

"It could be beautiful…"

"Yes, it has possibilities. But what do you have against the place?" He moved closer, but she

27

deliberately took several steps away. "Tell me the truth, please?"

"Oh, all right," she conceded. "I don't hate the place, really. In fact at one time I loved this land. And at one time I thought it might be mine."

"When?" Vincent seemed stunned by her revelation.

"Apparently just as you were bidding on it." She didn't look up to see his expression.

"What?" His large hand ran through the top of his brown hair, his confusion apparent.

Darien knew he'd never understand unless he had the facts. It was only fair to tell him. "I was looking into buying the land. Then when I'd finally gotten the financing in place, I was told I was too late. It had been optioned."

"I was never told anyone else was interested in it. I was given the impression it had been abandoned for years."

"It was. Three years to be exact."

"Did you know the people who lived here?"

"No. I never knew the...last owner. I just found out the lot was for sale and fell in love with it. By the time I was organized, it was sold. It's my own fault, really. If I'd moved more quickly, I might have gotten it." She drew a deep breath of the cooling air and tossed the charred wood bit aside, clapping her hand together to loosen the charcoal dust. "But it obviously wasn't meant to be mine. I do hope you'll be happy here, Vincent. It's a wonderful place."

"I never knew, Darien."

"It doesn't matter, really. I shouldn't have said anything. It's time you took me back to the city."

"In a minute," he stalled.

She figured he was trying to put all the fragments of information together and came up blank.

"Would you still like to live here?"

"No. It's your land and it's going to be your home. I'll find another place when it's meant to be." She stood tall and almost made herself believe it.

"Are you actively looking still?"

"Not recently. I got busy with work and my search kind of got lost for a while. In the spring I'll start again."

He followed her to the truck, and then hesitated at the passenger door. "Aren't you curious what I plan to do here?"

When she finally looked at him, she could only describe his look as pained. The emotion swamped her.

"No. Vincent, please take me home. You promised you would."

He closed her door and walked around the vehicle. They were both quiet until he made it back to the main road.

Pulling into a large chain gas station, he finally turned to her. "How about getting us some coffee for the ride back to the city while I top off the tank?" The distance did them both some good. By the time he joined her inside the small convenience store to pay for the gas, she was approaching the counter with two cups of coffee. She remembered how he took it from their short trip to the club after the auction.

"Hungry?" Darien shook her head no and moved away.

Back in the truck with the coffee open and in the holders, Vincent tried to break the ice. "How about finding us something on the radio?"

She wasn't sure what she'd choose, but she'd bet metal rock and roll wouldn't have been his first guess. Two songs later, he laughed aloud when the station mentioned they were listening to "classic" rock.

"Didn't realize you were that old, did you?" Darien said with a smile. She was back to the woman he'd met at the auction, her sadness put aside.

"I'm not sure I like being relegated into this "classic" category. I guess it happened around us."

While the rest of the trip was quiet, the tension had lessened. When he pulled up in front of her building without asking for her address, she finally smiled.

"Didn't stand much of a chance, did I? You've had access to me all along. If I'd known, I would have skipped brunch."

"And disappoint Sissy? Think of how we've improved her social standing in just a few hours." He realized immediately his joke didn't go over well.

"Sissy's social standing is not my concern and I'd prefer to be left off the agenda at all future meetings. I've spent the last eight years going out of my way to keep a clean reputation and I don't need Sissy or any of her gaggle of friends speculating about us." Darien realized she almost said tarnished, but that would have been wrong. At the moment she wasn't sure how to describe how she felt. Too many emotions were pulling in too many directions for her to think clearly.

"Darien, I don't care about social agendas. And my reputation isn't that bad, yet." His smile would be her undoing and almost was.

She moved closer and let her arms slide up around his neck. Her lips close to his, she let herself take the kiss she'd been dreaming about. His seat belt kept him locked in place and the absence of hers allowed her to move freely. When she finally released him, it was because she realized her fingers had been toying with the back of his hair. Her tongue had been probing into his mouth, tasting and learning, and worst of all, she felt a strange heat building inside her, one she couldn't control. Her nipples had budded under her silk shirt and her lower lips were heavy with a need she knew he'd created.

"Good-bye, Vincent. I hope you build a wonderful home at Millner's and that you have a great life there. Take care of yourself."

She slipped out before he could respond and didn't turn back. He sat a long time, she noted, watching through the peep hole, staring at the street level display window.

The large glass expanse was sparkling in the light, she knew, color reflecting back. Braided lengths of silk in rainbow colors screened the interior of the shop from the street. Several important pieces of pottery and crystal sat on wooden pillars, the minimalist suggestion there but not. It announced that Darien M. West saw customers by appointment only.

Chapter Three

"Damn the man," she said aloud in the empty elevator.

Darien walked with purpose into Vincent Leighton's outer office. She recognized his assistant, Mark, guarding entry into his boss's private domain. He glanced up, his expression one of recognition and surprise at her appearance in the office.

"Can I help you?"

"Is he in?" she asked, her words clipped, her attitude showing.

"Yes, but he's on the telephone. Do you have an appointment, Miss?"

"No. Is he alone?"

"Yes. If you'd care to have a seat, I'll let him know you're waiting."

She took purposeful steps past his desk and reached for the knob. "I'll tell him myself," she answered as she pushed open the door into Vincent's private office. Mark was around the desk seconds later, following her inside. His expression let his boss know he hadn't allowed her access.

Vincent glanced up. He nodded to Mark, who quietly pulled the door closed behind him.

"Something's come up; I'll get back to you tomorrow." The person on the other end of the call was dismissed with a minimum of conversation. After hanging up the phone, Vincent pushed back in his chair and watched her pace the length of his office. "Darien, to what do I owe the pleasure of this unscheduled meeting?" She stopped in place and turned, the look in her eyes flashing gold fire toward him. He watched as she took several controlling breaths before answering him.

In the short time she took to gather her thoughts, he took in the sight of her. Her hair was piled high on her head, but several curls had escaped their bonds, framing her face. It softened her look even though he realized it wasn't the look she was going for. "Darien?"

"Are you crazy? I mean completely, certifiably crazy?" She watched as he pushed back in the high-backed, leather swivel chair, further from the massive wood desk before him, crossing one long leg over the other ankle.

"Only occasionally that I know of." He tried to conceal a smile—this wasn't the time to laugh at her. He waited to see what approach she would take. Anger, it seemed, was her first.

"How could you do this to me? I've spent my entire career keeping my nose and my name clean. I know you less than two weeks and my reputation is in a shambles." She started pacing again.

"Maybe you should start by telling me just how I ruined your reputation?" The look she shot him would have had a lesser man running from the room. But Vincent took it in stride. He'd known there would be repercussions and this was just the beginning. He'd accept her anger and hopefully move past it.

"All right, Vincent, if that's how you want to play, you seem to be hell-bent on pushing my buttons. First my phone rang and I was introduced to Stan Woolard. You do know him?" He only acknowledged her with a nod. "Then he asked me if I could give him a rough timeframe for the new designs!" Again she tried for control, but the tremor in her voice gave away her anxiety. "The designs for Vincent Leighton's home." Studying him carefully, she noted he was still trying to conceal his smile.

"Not only was I taken by surprise, I wound up sounding like an idiot. I explained there must have been a mistake, but he went on to tell me you pulled the plug on his project until I had time to revise *his* plans!"

"Would you like coffee or soda?"

"Bite me, Vincent. I don't want anything from you, even coffee." She moved to the window and focused her attention on the traffic below. *"My* designs? You must be certifiably crazy." She shook her head in disbelief, and several more strands of curling hair fell down. "I tried to explain an error in communications, but he told me straight out there was no glitch, you directed him to take a step back and wait to be contacted by me when my designs were ready. And if that wasn't bad enough, he explained that he wasn't trying to push me, rather to understand my timeframe so he could rearrange his work schedule to accommodate me!" This time when she turned to him her anger had dissipated. "Do you have any idea how that makes me look, Vincent? Do you have any idea how rude this whole situation is?" She narrowed her eyes. "So help me, if you laugh at me now, I'll..."

Vincent slowly unfolded his length from the chair. The time it took him to reach her went by in slow motion for them both. His hands reached for her shoulders and she pulled back.

"Don't! Just stay away. I'm so frustrated with you right now I can't stand the sight of you." His heady laugh wasn't what she was prepared for. Once again, anger came to the forefront.

"You'll mellow. And in time you'll actually look forward to seeing me."

"In a pig's lifetime, Mr. Leighton." The words spilled from her lips and she turned her back, afraid she was doing just that: mellowing toward him when she wanted to be angry, wanted to keep the adrenaline pumping. "I'm not going to work on your house, especially now!" His hands stayed at his sides, but his chocolate eyes stared at her when she finally glanced back. "Fix this, Vincent. Call Stan and tell him it was all an error. I don't want anything to do with the project, or you. Understand?" She didn't wait for an answer. Instead she turned on her heel and pushed past him in a huff.

He followed her to the reception area where Mark watched her walk quickly toward the elevators. Finally Vincent broke out laughing, the confrontation over. He hoped with time she'd mellow toward him. "She sure knows how to make an entrance." When the elevator had swallowed her up, he turned back to his office.

He knew Mark was beyond confused. Vincent Leighton never acted like this with anyone, especially a woman. Vincent shook his head. Where would the situation lead?

****

Close to nine that night, the intercom rang in Darien's apartment. Immediately dread coursed through her. She wasn't expecting anyone. Hitting the button, she braced for the worst. "Yes?"

"Darien, can I come up?" Somehow she'd known it would be him, or had she hoped? It was a moot point now.

"Did you fix things with Stan Woolard?"

"That's what I'm here to discuss." There was an extended pause before he spoke again. "Would you prefer to discuss it over the intercom, or are you going to let me up?"

She didn't hold back the smile forming on her lips at his exasperated tone. Instead, she hit the buzzer to let him in. Only then did she pause to think about her appearance. She'd gone straight from his office to the gym, then come home and

35

showered, and pulled on old jeans and a sweatshirt. Her hair had air-dried and she wore no makeup. She was barefoot and was about to run to the bedroom to change when his fist pounded on the door. "Shoot, too late," she said aloud, slowly unlocking her front door.

Vincent Leighton stood leaning in the doorway, his tie long abandoned, his shirt unbuttoned at the neck. His jacket hung on him and his face told her he was tired. She couldn't find any words so she just took a step back to allow him into her private space. When he'd passed her, she turned to relock the door, taking a moment to compose herself. Turning back to him, she realized he hadn't gone into the apartment. Instead he stood watching her. His low wolf whistle surprised, thrilled, and annoyed her as he continued his slow appraisal of her appearance. She fought with her hands not to primp her curly hair and stood to her full height and stared. Neither said a word for a long time. Vincent broke the standoff.

"Darien, you look better than I've been imagining in my dreams."

A laugh worked its way toward her lips and she forced it back. "Why are you here, Vincent?" She nodded to the cardboard tube in his hand. "Are you a masochist?" The grin formed on her lips and she stopped short of biting her lower lip. She remembered how he'd taken over the last time she did.

"Yes, I suppose so. I have something to show you." He raised the tube toward her, but she didn't take it from him. She pushed past him and wandered into the open living area, Vincent following close behind her.

His initial reaction to her private space was subdued under the circumstances. He'd known she'd rented the two floors on a long-term lease in the four-story townhouse three years earlier and that the top two floor apartments were rented separately. She lived on the second floor; her showroom was the street level area.

He'd thought about what her living environment might look like, but the space before him wasn't what he expected. To his left was the living and dining area, the large front windows covered in several layers of sheer curtains and heavier drapes. Walls of vivid sea blue reflected green, depending on the light. Her furniture was overstuffed and comfortable looking. She'd used lots of tapestry and tweed fabric, sturdy and long lasting. Only accents such as throw pillows and afghans softened the room. Her mix of old and new lamps and tables invited him to relax and get comfortable. Her dining room was open to the space, the trestle table flanked by eight chairs that didn't match yet resided easily around the wood. The kitchen was behind it, a half wall serving as a bar area and room divider. It wasn't a large space, but it used the square footage to full advantage. White cabinets hung against walls painted a lighter green.

Vincent could only assume her bedroom and bath were down the small hallway to his right, but even he didn't have the nerve to wander there uninvited, yet. He swelled slightly at the thought of her and a bed, the combination a heady idea he'd had stuck in the back of his mind since first seeing her. Somehow he wanted to see her stretched across the center of a huge bed, her hair spread over the pillows, her arms reaching to him. In his mind, she was naked. His hands were reaching to touch her in a way that only two adults can understand when the connection is right.

"Five minutes..." They eyed each other carefully before he turned to the left and went to the dining area. He took the crystal vase full of orange and yellow mums from the center of the table and thrust it toward her before pulling the plans from the tube and spreading them on the center of the wooden expanse. He looked around for something to hold down the corners of the rolling pages. Darien, after huffing an exasperated breath, left him and returned shortly with several small leather beanbags. She tossed them to him one at a time as he smoothed out the pages, weighting each corner. There was an obvious hesitation then before she moved toward him.

Vincent had hoped her curiosity would win out and he was right. Slowly she approached, her eyes trained on him. She looked at him dead on for a few seconds before turning her attention to the plans. Darien surprised him when her hands encircled his waist. What he hoped would be an introduction toward intimacy turned out to be her pushing him out of her way to get a better look. She moved closer to the table and pulled out the chair he had stood behind. Darien said nothing, only looked at the plans. After several minutes she left her spot and turned on brighter lights in the room, including the medieval-looking chandelier over the table. Again she studied what he put in front of her.

"What's wrong with it, other than being too modern for the site?"

"Modern or contemporary. it leaves me cold. I hate it."

"Then why didn't you tell Stan before it went this far?" This time she did look to him for an honest answer.

"The design just sort of snowballed out of control."

Darien threw back her head and laughed. "Somehow, I don't see you as the type to be steamrolled into something you don't like." She studied him more intently, her cheeks heating before she turned away.

He would have loved to know what she was thinking at that precise moment.

"I suppose I should correct that and say I allowed it to happen because I didn't really care at the time."

"And now?"

"I've realized it's a lot of money and time to waste on something I won't be comfortable in." He pulled out the dining chair beside her, pausing only to tug off his jacket. Sitting heavily, he rolled back his sleeves. The lack of space between their bodies, shoulder to shoulder, didn't escape either of them.

"What did you originally want? You must have given Stan some idea of where to start?"

Vincent brought out a few sketches on yellow paper and passed them to her. She studied them carefully before speaking. "How did you get from this"—she held the yellow page out—"to this? The differences are overwhelming. We're talking about two entirely different home plans."

"What did you see, Darien? It's important to me. Please tell me what you saw when you looked at the site. You must have visualized something or the land wouldn't have captured your imagination and your heart." Until meeting her, a building site was just a site. Now, after seeing it through her eyes, he understood much more. This was a place to set down roots and build a home for his wife and family. That she kept coming back as his visual wife had bothered him greatly at first. He'd resigned himself to the idea it might not happen, but it might. Either way, the land deserved better than a bored rendition of other people's ideas.

"What I saw doesn't matter..."

"It does to me; I saw it on your face when we were there Sunday. Please show me?"

For a long time they sat beside each other

quietly. Ultimately, Darien left him alone, disappearing for a long time. Just when he thought she might not come back she was behind him, pulling out sketches she'd done. Darien handed them to him, then walked away purposefully. In the kitchen she pulled out a bottle of sparkling water, splashed some into two glasses on the bar, adding ice and lime slices before going back. Vincent accepted the glass with a nod but didn't speak; his eyes were trained on her concept of the home she would have put on the site.

"It's beautiful, Darien. Very Frank Lloyd Wright mixed with twenties farmhouse." She took the seat beside him once again and studied Stan's plans. "I like the arts and craft style much better than this modern glass and metal concept. It left me cold. Yours looks like a home."

"Why let it get so far from your original concept? It's your home, your money. Why didn't you lead Stan back toward your vision?" This time she watched him intently, trying to figure him out or at least get a point of reference on him. His brown eyes drew her to him; she wanted to touch him, to feel his warmth. She didn't, of course, but the pull was strong, so strong it all but frightened her on a primal level.

"I suppose because it didn't matter that much then. Now it does. When I realized just how much it does mean to me, I pulled the plug with Stan."

"I don't like the timing of this, Vincent. If we hadn't met, would you have let him go ahead?"

"I don't honestly know. But now I realize I want something more, something I'll be content in. Something a family would be comfortable in."

"What do you want from me?" she asked, afraid to let her mind wander too far from the moment. It never entered her mind he might have a woman on the side, so to speak. Or was she the one on the side?

She refocused on the conversation, somewhat disappointed with the reality she'd acknowledged might truly exist. She looked away from him, afraid her feelings would surface. The intense look on his face made her ignore the unknown.

"Can you fix it?" he asked, after a longer pause that seemed to drill through her soul.

"Fix it?" She stood and walked away laughing, thankful to put space between them. Darien had witnessed chemistry between people but never felt it for herself. If this was any inclination toward that road, she was in deep. "Fix it! Vincent, you're talking about re-designing from the ground up."

"But you could do it, if you wanted to?"

"Do you really expect me to design you a house with no notice and no real thought behind it? It would be as bad as Stan's in some ways, worse in others."

"Couldn't you just sketch it so he'd understand where I was trying to go with it originally, just so I could re-direct him?" Vincent watched as she ran both hands through her hair.

The man was completely insane. He was technically a total stranger. Rich and handsome, yes; crazy as a loon, definitely. And if he hadn't looked at her with those brown puppy-dog eyes, she might have stood a chance. In an instant she knew she'd try, mainly because of the land and its history, and begrudgingly, she admitted to herself, to please Vincent Leighton.

"I must be as crazy as you are." Darien shook her head again, then all but ordered him to move aside. "I need to be here," she added, softening her tone.

He was slightly taken aback by her attitude but relinquished his seat, watching her spread all the plans on the table. The onslaught of questions she tossed at him for the next two hours boggled his mind. Eventually she put aside her notes to scan the plans in front of her. She left him, returning shortly with paper and pencils in hand. Darien seemed to forget he was there for a time. No music played in the background and the television wasn't turned on. The only noise in the space was the din of traffic below them. Vincent didn't mind, he loved the undercurrent hum of the city. And apparently she did too. It seemed that when she had work on her mind, she could tune out the world and him, though he stood just across the room from her.

It wasn't until her stomach rumbled that she looked up and saw him staring out the window. She moved quietly to the kitchen, returning with two Creamsicles. He took the ice cream she offered without question or comment, and then turned to watch her.

She was a sight, he told himself as he pulled back the paper wrapper. He couldn't remember the last time he'd had an ice-cream pop. She nibbled at the top of her pop, and then let her tongue slide over the sides. He hardened at the sight of her and turned away. When he ventured a look back, the ice cream was gone, but she still chewed on the stick. She leaned over the table, one foot on the floor, one knee braced on the chair beside her. The pose was familiar and he remembered the photograph. She was bent over the plans with several pencils stuck behind her ear. Stretching to pull forward one of his pages, the sweater she wore clung to her breast and smoothed to her slim waist. He knew she wasn't a small woman. No, she was very well proportioned. Her hourglass figure only enhanced the denim-covered long length of leg.

A shiver ran through his body and it wasn't from the ice cream. Thoughts of touching her made him tingle with an ache of need and frustration. He glanced at his watch and realized it was after midnight. Since Darien was lost over the plans and he didn't want to interrupt her, he stretched out on her couch, his hands behind his head. He just wanted a few minutes to close his eyes before he left. Through half-closed eyes he watched her movements, graceful and smooth. She chewed on the pop stick when she was working through a problem. He wanted to pull her down next to him and just hold her for a few minutes. His eyes closed somewhere during this thought.

Darien stretched to her full height and let her lips curl into a smile. The hours had flown by, but the end result was worth the work. Before her lay the combination of all three designs. Somehow she felt it was right for the site and would be enhanced by the surrounding grounds. In the back of her mind she knew how the gardens should be planted and didn't resist pulling another empty page forward to quickly sketch her vision. When she finally dropped the pencil, she stretched her arms above her had and rotated her neck a few times. Only then did she realize he was still there.

Vincent had become extraneous once the process started. Now, watching him sleep on her sofa, she allowed herself to openly look at him. He was tall and well-proportioned with defined thigh muscles under his Brooks Brothers pants. His white shirt still looked somewhat fresh, considering he'd worn it all day and had now slept in it for...at least six hours, she realized, checking the clock. She restrained her initial urge to run her hand over his cheek. Self-preservation alone made her move away to make coffee before she touched him. The one thing Darien knew was that one touch wouldn't be enough.

Not now, not after seeing what he envisioned for his home. It was a strange, intimate act to design for a person, but to willingly give Vincent her house design for this particular land was beyond intense.

She'd given him a small piece of herself. She didn't want to know if or when he'd realize her gift.

With a slight ache she let herself imagine what it might be like to live there with him. The idea became a blurry visual, too perfect to be real, and the direction her thoughts were taking scared her. She moved to the master bath, but the quick shower she took didn't wake her as she'd hoped. Instead, it seemed to lull her toward a much-needed sleep. At least she didn't have to be anywhere until this afternoon. She'd wake him up and send him on his way, then crawl between the cool sheets and sleep for a few hours.

Wearing clean jeans and a cotton tee, she let the idea of a bra fade out of and then back into her mind, taking the shirt hem up and over her arms, struggling into a bra and smoothing the shirt back down. While one side of her was mischievous enough to want to present herself to him without it just to see his reaction, she knew it would be opening a door she wasn't ready to walk through. The scent of brewing coffee found her, negating any other ideas.

****

Darien stood beside the sofa, a coffee mug in her hand. She didn't want to wake him, yet she wanted him out of her space. Kneeling beside him, she gently touched his shoulder. He woke with a start but only smiled when he saw her. Slowly his arms unfolded from behind his head as he stretched.

"What time is it?" he whispered, reaching to take the mug from her hands. She offered it easily as he shifted only enough to drink from it before handing it back.

"Just after six," she told him, waiting for his reaction.

"Too early, Darien." Vincent's arm reached forward and again took the mug. Instead of drinking from it, he put it on the floor to the side of the sofa.

His hand caught her around the waist and pulled her down beside him. She started to fight him, but his other arm came over her, settling her in place. "Just lie with me for a few minutes," he whispered.

Vincent felt her body go from rigid to accepting and finally to comfortable in his arms. It was a tight fit for them both to be lying side by side but he didn't care and as she shifted against him, bringing one leg over his, he decided she didn't either. She felt too good in his arms, right for him in all the right places. She was sturdy beside him, warm and alive. His mind wandered in its sleepy haze, thinking about what she would feel like under him. His erection suddenly strained against his zipper. Darien curled tighter against him and sighed. He tried willing his body to let go of the thought of being buried inside her, but her arm came across his chest, pressing her tighter to him.

"At least you don't snore," she whispered just before she let herself drift off to sleep. When he'd pulled her down, she'd started to squirm to get away, but that had only made the situation worse. She could feel him growing against her. His expanding manhood sent a thrill through her. Ultimately, she'd given up and allowed him to hug her to his warm body. For his benefit or for hers? She decided she didn't care. Darien just wanted to feel for a change. His heart beat beneath her cheek, the rhythm lulling her to snuggle tighter against him. God, he felt good, warm and safe. Yet she understood he wouldn't be safe. Instead he'd make her life crazy. At the moment she didn't care. She just wanted to be with him.

Vincent came awake when she shifted from his body, the cool air surrounding him foreign after having her next to him. He stretched, but didn't let go of her.

"What time is it?"

"It's after seven. You have to go," she answered, but she didn't get up. Instead she carefully turned her back to him, waited for him to shift further back in the cushions, and spooned up against him. It was easy to let his arms fall back around her. "Just for a minute," she told him, and promptly dropped back to sleep.

Vincent didn't fall back; instead he tried to control his breathing and his mind. Having Darien pushed back against him with his arms wrapped around her was not conducive to sleep. His fingers brushed the top of her full breast and he stopped himself. When he touched her, he wanted her to be awake and aware of him feeling her, taking every stroke and caress with the full meaning he was giving it. He knew it would happen. It would take longer than he'd originally thought, but after last night he knew she'd be his. It didn't shock or surprise him that in his mind he was assuming for the long haul.

He'd met women who had seen him in their visions of long-term, but until Darien M. West, he'd never felt it for himself. Vincent decided he'd need to tread carefully if he wanted to make her his, permanently. Though his fingers still longed to feel her nipple come to life between them, he contented himself with nuzzling in her long, still-damp, hair.

He realized she'd showered sometime while he slept; only a thin T-shirt and lacy bra separated them. His erection pulsed back to life and he knew he couldn't stay with her this way without taking it a step or two further. He drew in a deep breath and laughed lightly. Hell, who was he kidding? If he stayed beside her any longer he'd take her, one way or another. The knowledge that he wanted their first time together to be more than a hurried morning made him finally move, waking her gently with his lips to her cheek.

"Darien, wake up, honey, it's after eight." His lips caressed her cheek and moved toward her ear. "Darien, we have to get up." His words woke her. She stretched like a contented cat alongside him. As she came awake and felt him, she all but jumped from the couch. His arms held her steady until she woke completely. "At least you're not used to waking up beside a man..." He let his lips trail to the soft spot behind her ear, not resisting the urge to run his tongue back and forth several times.

Darien carefully moved from his arms, trying to figure out how to salvage some pride in the process. She stood slowly and moved to the window, opening the curtains all the way, flooding the room with morning light. Her hands rose in a full stretch and came down on her head, dragging her hair from her face.

Vincent sat on the side of the sofa to gather his thoughts. He left her quietly, returning with a fresh cup of hot coffee and handed it to her before disappearing down the hallway.

She didn't move. Didn't want to offer to make him breakfast. Suddenly didn't want him in her space. He was back behind her, lifting the mug from her hand, drinking deeply from it. When he handed it back, he moved away and started to unroll his shirt sleeves. He grabbed his jacket from the dining room chair, pausing to watch her.

"I'll pick you up at seven," he started.

She laughed aloud. "No, you won't." Darien crossed the length of the room toward him, knowing he was watching. She knew her nipples were budded into large raspberries under her shirt, but refused to cross her arms in front to cover her arousal, rather stood tall and proud before him. Standing several feet away from him, she pulled his cardboard tube from the center of the table. Neatly stacked beside it was a plastic tray of colored pencils and markers.

Rulers and assorted drawing tools lay beside it.

There were several sheets of paper crumpled beside them. Accepting the tube, he caught her eye and held it, still amazed at the green color staring back. "Did you sleep at all?" She smiled and nodded, then glanced back to the couch. "Can I look at these?"

"Of course, but not here. I have work to do today, and I'm already behind schedule. It's time you left, Vincent." He didn't look away and neither did she.

"All right, I won't push my luck." He tapped the tube against his empty palm several times, deciding how to handle her. She laughed once again as if she could read his mind and he knew that was the problem. He kept trying to handle her. "When will you see me again?" He took a step closer and she drew a deep breath.

"That's not a good idea," Darien told him with the shake of her shoulder.

"I think it's a great idea. Besides I owe you for this. Have dinner with me?" Darien's eyes flashed, gold specks forming around the ice green centers. She was mad, but he wasn't exactly certain why. She took several controlled breaths and crossed her arms in front of her.

"Vincent, that is my gift to you; no repayment is necessary. No suppers, no flowers, no gifts. I did this as much for me as for you. I did it because it was right for the land. Can you understand that?" She watched as it dawned on him how much she loved that land.

"Darien, all this work, the thought and time." She cut him off mid-sentence.

"Closed subject. I hope whatever you decide to build will be comfortable for you, but I want no part of it from here on out. And don't get too far ahead of yourself. That's not a complete set of drawings there.

Just a few sketches to work from."

"I didn't expect a complete set of mechanical drawings, Darien, but you've given me your plan."

"As a gift. Now, my gift back is for you to leave. I have work today and I'm already behind schedule."

Vincent stared, trying not to smile, knowing it would infuriate her. Instead he decided he needed to touch her, that contact would make her rethink her decision. She was so close, within an arm's reach in one step. With a second step his empty hand encircled her waist and closed the distance between their bodies. Her hand with the coffee mug moved to the side so as not to slosh the contents on him as he let his head drop to hers, capturing her lips in the kiss he'd dreamed about. She didn't resist; instead she parted her lips to accept his tongue into her mouth, tasting him mixed with the coffee flavor. Her free hand came up to his cheek, her fingers spreading over his stubbly chin before pulling back.

"Have you ever worn a beard?" Her normally husky voice sounded wistful, strangled with want and lust.

His dark eyes flashed at a thought recognized by them both and he couldn't stop the involuntary twitch in his groin as he imagined teasing her skin. "Years ago, but it didn't fit the professional image."

She only nodded and he wondered if she'd accept a full beard, dark and softly caressing her skin as he kissed.

"Want me to grow it back, see if you like it?"

"Not just now," she told him, as she directed his lips back to hers, hating him and herself. But she wanted one last taste of him, a memory to cherish, she decided as she sought more of the passion he made her feel.

Vincent pulled away after shifting her to cradle his growing interest. They both felt his need and her kisses were conveying her desires as her hips gently rotated against him. He groaned and she moved away.

"Are you going to have dinner with me tonight?"

"No, tomorrow, after seven-thirty." He held her eye. Was she pushing him back as a power play, or did she really have plans? And if she had plans, who were they with? The whole idea started to frustrate him, so he turned away.

"I'll pick you up, tomorrow night, seven-thirty." He drank in a long look at her while she unlocked the door. "Thanks for this..." He waved the tube once in the air.

"Don't thank me until you see them." Her smile made his fingers itch to tear open the tube, but he knew he wouldn't. "Go home, Vincent," she said, her voice low, with little resistance.

He didn't acknowledge the vulnerability he heard in her tone. "Good night, Darien." The back of his hand brushed her cheek and her eyes automatically closed. "Oh, God, Darien, do you have any idea what you do to me?" With her eyes still downcast, she didn't answer. "Tomorrow..."

She closed the door quietly and waited for several seconds before she allowed her body to slip down its glossy finish until she was resting on the polished wood floor. Only then did she permit herself to really wonder what it would be like when they made love. And she knew now it would happen. When and where, she hoped to be able to control. But it was inevitable that she'd take him as her lover. She jumped to her feet and made a beeline for her bed, hoping to relive his touch in her dreams.

Chapter Four

"Damn," he whispered to himself. Having been late to the office, he couldn't put off the staff who had already gathered, very uneasily waiting for him. He was never late. He tried to dispense with the agenda as quickly as possible. The tube on the windowsill was calling to him. Time went against him the rest of the day. Between meetings and phone calls, he hadn't a minute to spare. Vincent knew the moment he opened the tube everything else around him would be lost.

It was after eight when he finally walked into his apartment and spread the plans on his dining room table. He tossed his jacket on a chair and rolled back his sleeves. For a long time he stared at the page on top. It was a very rough drawing of her idea, only it had changed from her original concept. This page reflected some of her ideas as well as the general shape of Stan's concept. Only now his preference influenced the overall appearance.

He forced himself into a hot shower, grabbing a beer from the kitchen on his way back to the dining room. The whole time he'd stood under the hot water, all he visualized was the house and the new look she'd given to it. Refreshed, he pulled the original plans aside and put his original sketches beside it. Next to them he put the single page she'd included from her original concept. Below them on the table sat the new plan, a compilation of all three. Somehow it all worked and he felt like a kid. The excitement when he first saw the land came back in a rush.

"I'll be a son of a bitch," he said out loud, and laughed. She'd known, down to the last window, what he was looking for. He stood abruptly, realizing it was mostly what she'd been wanting. Somehow it didn't matter; this concept was much more appealing than what might have been built. The pages behind it reflected some minor changes, but he understood she'd left the footprint of the building basically intact.

Only several major changes had been incorporated. The master suite was larger, as was the downstairs den. He smiled when he saw the room sketched, and in bold black letters, the word "BAR" printed. At least she kept her sense of humor. He shuffled through the rest of the pages, each one a bare-bones idea of what it could look like. When he came to the last sheet, he realized it was a concept for the gardens with a pool area and cabana. This was a place he could live, where he'd be comfortable. Now he just had to figure out how to get Darien to live there with him.

****

She was dressed and waiting when he arrived. He hit the intercom and she buzzed him up. Checking the floral arrangement on the back of the upright piano, she smiled at the assorted colored tulips, wondering where he found spring flowers in November. Then she remembered she was dealing with Vincent Leighton. He could obtain just about anything he wanted. How he'd known they were her favorite was still a mystery. His knock was much lighter than it had been two nights earlier. As she opened the door she tried to prepare herself for the sight of him. It didn't work. She found herself letting out a similar wolf whistle to the one he'd graced her with at their last meeting.

Standing in the hallway in a dark blue suit with a lighter blue shirt, his patterned tie dragging her eyes upward to his face, she knew all was lost. His grin said it all, confidence and arrogance rolled into one. Now she hated herself for being nervous about their date. Stepping back to let him in, she stilled under his watchful eye. The plum-colored dress set off her eyes, the material hugging her body. Apparently, from the gleam in his eye, Vincent agreed. She cleared her throat before attempting to speak.

"Thank you for the tulips. They're beautiful." When she thought to let it drop she found she couldn't. "How did you know?" His eyes met hers and he smiled.

"I didn't. I only knew roses would have been too common for you."

"Thank you," she managed, annoyed at the blush creeping up her cheeks. Why was she always blushing around him? It didn't matter. Her feelings went a lot deeper than she was willing to accept or acknowledge at this point in time.

"Are you ready to go?"

"Yes, I'll get my coat."

His tone had sounded harsh to his ears, his nerves pushing forward, but then she returned, wrapped in a black wool overcoat with a green and gold scarf twisted at her neck. The colors reflected her eyes and he smiled at her before taking her hand. He stood beside her while she locked the door, and kept her hand in his while waiting for the elevator and during the ride.

Outside, his car was parked by the curb. The driver closed them in the warmth of the back seat and apparently knew their destination. It didn't take long for Darien to realize why. He was taking her to his apartment. She didn't hide the skeptical look that crossed her face.

"You live here." It was a statement of fact, not a question.

"Yes."

"Why are you bringing me here?" This time her voice gave away her angst.

"Do you trust me?" He held her eye and waited for an answer. She shook her head and laughed.

"Somewhat against my better judgment," she acknowledged. He returned her laugh and smiled a smile that made her insides warm and heat course through her veins. It was a good thing he held her hand or she might have reached to touch him.

"Something I want to show you," was all he told her by way of explanation.

****

Darien slipped out of her coat, draping it over a center hall table, unwrapping the scarf as she walked inside.

"Make yourself at home, if you can..."

His comment confused her. She threaded the silk through her hands as she wandered ahead into the main living room. Standing on the threshold of the room, she paused to take it all in. While formal, it had high ceilings and wonderful moldings. The wall of windows gave way to a magnificent view of the Manhattan skyline. Yet it was all so nondescript. The elements were there, but it was bland. Now she started to understand him. Darien was aware he was close behind her. His body heat radiated toward her as his hands came up to stroke her shoulders from behind.

"What about it don't you like?"

He hesitated before he answered, an acknowledgment that it was important. "It's not that I don't like it really, it's just..."

"Vincent, don't make me put words to your thoughts. Tell me."

"I suppose its fine really, just formal. It doesn't invite me to come and sit and enjoy the view. Even in my own home I've never put my feet up on the coffee table." His laugh was genuine. Darien relaxed back against him.

"Did you have it done?"

"No, God, no. It was like this when I found it. Turnkey complete, just move in my clothes and I was done. Only it's all so…tan!" They laughed together at his accurate description.

"Are you trying to tell me you need a little color in your life, Mr. Leighton?"

"That depends on how and where you want to put it."

"I'll think on it and get back to you." She started to turn toward him, wanted to reach up and kiss him. He let her turn back, but didn't let her go. "Is the whole apartment the same?"

"Basically."

"How long have you lived here?"

"Three years." This time she pulled from his embrace and turned to stare at him.

"Three years you've lived in this space you're so uncomfortable with?"

"I don't spend much time here; generally I'm in the bedroom or the study. This is more of a pass-through."

"An expensive pass-through. Can I see the bedroom and study?" She took a few steps back into the living room, turning around several times, taking a long look around. When she caught him watching her, she started to laugh at the intense look on his face. She paused only to drop her scarf along the back of an overstuffed club chair covered in tan silk. The simple swatch of green and gold shimmered in the low light. Catching the look in his eyes, she added, "Don't even think about going there, Vincent. This is simply a tour."

He nodded his understanding and directed her down the hallway to the right, opening several doors as they passed. The staid guest suites didn't impress her. Vincent stopped beside the open doorway to the study, and watched her wander into the tan space and get a feel for the room.

She bit back a smile, and joined him in the hallway, after taking a quick glance at the overloaded desk area and the huge plasma television on the far wall. Here was a look of being lived in, the sofa long with slightly crumpled cushions, magazines and books stacked on the coffee table. In the far corner was a small yet elegant wet bar.

The last door was open and she immediately tried to pull back a laugh. From the hallway she could see tan silk paper covering the walls. Once inside she confirmed what she thought. "It's all quite tan, isn't it?" she started, before finally letting herself take the release she'd been holding back. Somehow her nerves dissipated with the laugh and she wasn't so uptight being this close to Vincent, especially in his apartment and now in his master bedroom. Darien walked further into the room. "It's not a bad space; it's just kind of...dull."

"I know."

She knew he watched her wander through his bedroom and into his bath. When his eyes closed she wondered if he was envisioning her lying across the king-sized bed, her hair sprawled behind her on the pillow, then realized it was her fantasy.

"Not so much anymore with you standing in it." He cleared his throat before adding, "Come, I'll see about supper." He held out his hand.

Darien knew the longer she spent in his room with a large bed that close by, the harder it would be to leave. And he was trying to give her time. Darien understood and followed him quickly.

****

The kitchen was the only room in the house that had any personality. Copper pots hung from an overhead rack, jars and canisters lined the counters.

Stainless steel, restaurant-style equipment took precedence in the space but fit with the terra-cotta floor tiles and hand-painted Mexican ceramics on the backsplashes. Vincent pulled off his jacket and draped it over a barstool across from one of the work areas. He was rolling back his sleeves as he walked to the refrigerator.

"What would you like to drink—water, soda, or something hot?"

Darien ran her fingers along the cold counter and smiled, speaking her thoughts before she changed her mind. "You mean you're not going to try and ply me with wine?" She spun around, batting her eyelashes in over-the-top mock flirting.

"No, I think I'm on enough thin ice without giving you a headache. However, I do have a lovely white. It's fruity yet crisp."

"Water for now. Maybe I'll sample your wine with supper."

He winked, pulled out a bottle of Pellegrino water, and set it in front of her, along with the wine. "Can you work on this while I get the grill going?" It wasn't an order so much as a practical way to get both things done. Before she could answer, he continued, "Corkscrew in the drawer under the far cabinet, glasses above."

He moved with a practiced ease in the space and she wasn't surprised. Somehow when she entered the room, she knew this was the place he'd made his own. The task actually relaxed her and she took the opportunity to turn on the radio that hung from an overhead cabinet. It came on to a fifties rock station and she left it. With ice in her water glass, she rounded the island to bring him his wine. He accepted it, returning her smile.

"The kitchen wasn't finished when you moved in, was it?"

His head turned quickly and he laughed with

her. "A water leak from the apartment above. When I saw it, only the counters and cabinets were in place. I had to pick the flooring and the tile." He sipped from his glass before turning his attention back to the steaks he was seasoning. "How did you know?"

"Easy. There's actually some color in here."

"Yes, well, don't let it relax you. Those few decisions took years off my life and drove me crazy."

This close, Darien didn't resist the urge to let her fingers lightly stroke the few graying hairs at his temple. "Why not change it over the years?" She moved away, pulling a cutting board forward on the counter. Without much thought, she picked up a knife and started mincing garlic for their Caesar salad after surveying the ingredients Vincent had laid out. It was automatic to head to the refrigerator and pull out a small bottle of oiled sardines from the door shelf. She started to mash them against some salt she'd sprinkled with the garlic using the back of a wooden spoon.

Vincent watched her for a moment. When he realized she'd caught him staring, he moved away and pulled open a pantry drawer. He washed potatoes, his back to her, before finally answering. "I suppose it wasn't a priority at the time. I live alone and don't entertain here often. I've left it up to the caterer to handle the few times I have. Bring in some flowers and such. With twenty people it isn't so dull anymore."

"Has it become a priority now, Vincent?" She moved beside him, deciding which bottle of imported olive oil she wanted to use. He was slicing the potatoes into thick wedges.

"Not at the moment, I just wanted you to understand me a little better."

"And tactfully letting me see you know your way around a kitchen is part of the process?" She liked that he had the good sense not to cover his embarrassment. She wasn't prepared for him to pull her to him and kiss her senseless.

"I'd think twice before doing that in a public place, Darien. And I didn't want to have to think tonight."

"Oh," was all she managed to utter before she moved away in self-defense.

The deep-fryer beeped ready and he dropped the steaks on the grill portion of the cooktop after lowering the basket into the fryer. Satisfied they were on schedule, he pulled her to him and held her close, not quite dancing to the song on the radio. When it ended, he released her, immediately going back to their preparations. They set the table in relative silence except for directions to supplies or preferences.

Vincent refilled his wine glass and put the bottle in front of Darien, letting her make the decision. What could have been uncomfortable turned into an enjoyable meal. Their conversation was light and the food good. She was woman enough to tell him so. Toward the end of their meal, she sampled the wine.

"It's light and crisp," she said after several small sips, then went back to her water.

When the dishes were stacked, he pulled her back to the study while coffee brewed. On the desk he pulled the plans forward, lightly pushing her down into the chair behind the desk.

"What do you see here?" He leaned over her and pointed to the entry. "Wood or steel for the front door?" For the next hour and a half, they picked each room apart. Darien made notes as they went, filling in details she pulled from him without him realizing he was designing the interior. They went through several cups of coffee and a plate of exquisite chocolate chip cookies.

She learned that two days a week, his cleaning

woman came in and regularly left him a treat. Today it was cookies. When Darien finally dropped the pencil and stretched, she realized it was after eleven. She also knew she'd given herself away with the garden sketch. She'd made it a spring garden, with tulips by the hundreds framing the walkway.

"Vincent, I give up. My mind is boggled." She watched as he rubbed his temples with long, sturdy fingers.

"I didn't mean to turn this into a marathon. I just had a few questions. Come, I'll take you home." He reached for her hand and she gave it, allowing him to pull her up from the chair.

She wound up very close to his body and mentally prepared herself for what might come. What she got was a quick peck of his lips on her cheek and his hand drawing her toward the doorway. Their ride was quiet, Darien slightly stunned at his lack of physical contact. She was disappointed when he'd done exactly what she asked him to. He'd given her space and not put her in an awkward position. Darien loved and hated him at the same time. He walked her to her apartment, moving inside easily with her.

"Would you like coffee?" she asked as she pulled off her coat.

"No." He looked at her and let his lips curl into a strange smile. "Darien, did I follow your rules tonight, no pressure, did you feel safe?"

"Yes," she answered, hesitant because of his smile.

"And you're home safely?"

"Yes. Vincent, what's on your mind?"

His grin widened and he took a step toward her. In response she took a step back. With two more moves her back was literally against a wall, just where he'd wanted her. Vincent watched as her eyes flashed with recognition. Slowly, he moved his hands to hers, drawing her arms upwards. She thought he'd drop them on his shoulders, and was cautious as he drew them up along the wall, over her head.

Just before his lips descended on hers, he whispered, "All bets are off, Darien." This was the kiss she thought she might get in his den, the kiss that opened a doorway. One of his hands dropped to her waist, but his other hand still held hers up against the wall, their fingers entwined. With his lips still fixed to hers, his tongue tasting and exploring her, his hand moved from her waist around her back and tugged her body to him, his need apparent. A small groan worked through her, coming out as more of a strangled moan. Vincent's fingers massaged her buttocks, his pressure forcing her over his hardness. When he had her in place, he let his hand wander up her back and finally around to capture her breast. It filled his palm and he groaned.

She'd wanted him to just kiss her, but now her nipple had come to life under his fingertips and she wanted more. Darien arched closer, letting out a small involuntary whimper. He dropped her wrists and found her other breast, kneading them both while his tongue swirled around hers in a heady combination of want and need.

She felt a growl work its way up through his chest, could feel the rumblings inside him as he pulsed against her just before he turned away, swearing. With his back to her he finally spoke.

"Damn it, Darien, how do you always make me forget my self-control?" When she didn't answer, he spun around. "God, Darien, how is it I lived before I knew you?"

Again, she didn't answer; rather she stayed against the wall, still trying to catch her breath.

His voice softened as he moved closer. She didn't shy away; she looked him in the eye. Vincent let his tongue slide along her fingers before she moved them from her face to accept his second kiss. The kiss was different, controlled. "This isn't finished, Darien. It's only a start. I'll call you..." was all he managed to say before he left.

Darien waited several minutes before pushing herself away from the wall and locking the door. She knew no truer words had been spoken between them. This was a beginning for them; it was the ultimate end that frightened her.

Chapter Five

"Ugh," Darien uttered at the sight of her blinking answering machine. She'd had little sleep, ultimately tugging the extra pillow to her chest, holding it tightly as she remembered how he danced her around his kitchen, how he looked at her in the car on the way back to her apartment. And most importantly, how he'd pushed her against the wall and kissed her until the heat seeped from her body. The idea that he could make her melt with a kiss was intimidating, to say the least.

For a woman who always kept her mind clear and her heart unencumbered, Darien was lost. She hadn't wanted any part of him in her life, yet here he was, just a few weeks after their first meeting, distracting her from her normal life and sleep patterns. It was so much easier to survive when emotions didn't interfere. In the past she enjoyed male companionship, but was always able to leave it in a neat compartment, something to be brought out and played with on occasion.

She understood it wasn't a productive way to form any long-term relationships. That had been her goal. The men she saw were all respectable businessmen who accepted the limits she put on the time they spent together. When their need changed, they moved on. Darien was proud of the fact she didn't hesitate when she ran into any of them. They were always friendly and attentive because she never let a relationship end on a sour note. It was easy when you didn't have anything invested. Now, without realizing it, she'd invested a lot in Vincent

Leighton. This wasn't a feeling she was comfortable with.

Hitting the button on her way past the machine, she listened to the mechanical voice tell her she had several messages. The first two were business, nothing important. The third had her halting in her steps toward the freezer. Vincent Leighton's voice filled her empty home, though she thought he sounded different. Tired maybe? His words—and his attitude—turned her cold.

"Darien, I'll be away on business for a few days, probably a week. I'll call you when I get back."

Staid, professional, and a duty call, she decided after listening to it several times. Her ice pop was long gone from her mind as well as the thought of any food right then. She stripped on her way through the apartment, standing under the hot spray, hoping it would wash away the feeling of doom that spread through her with his message. He had chosen to use her home machine, not her cell phone, therefore bypassing the opportunity to speak directly with her. Toweling dry, she decided it was for the best.

Her relationship with Vincent, no matter how short, was beginning to interfere with her everyday life. She found her stomach knotting every time her cell rang today, disappointed when it wasn't him. His touch made her think about things she knew wouldn't materialize: a future together or sharing the house out east, making their relationship permanent, starting a family. Just the fact that her mind had gone in that direction worried her.

Darien had known all her life she was different from most girls, and, later the women she knew. Her size forced her to make choices early on and she'd stuck with them. Her schooling was more important than dating, especially since none of the boys in her high school were anywhere near her height. At least not until her junior year, when she started to notice them. But by then she'd garnered the reputation of being distant and bookish. Using it as her best defense, she hid herself away with textbooks and extra classes. When she got to college, the boys were finally taller, but her confidence was lacking. Again, it was easier to throw herself into her studies than to experiment with live boys.

In the first years after graduation, she'd forced herself to concentrate on her career. Those few years had turned into a way of life. When her thirtieth birthday passed last summer, she'd taken stock of herself and her life. Liking what she'd accomplished professionally, Darien understood it was at the expense of her private life. Now, at the worst possible time, along came Vincent Leighton.

It seemed that after getting what he wanted from her, he'd slip back into his normal routine. He had a new concept for his house; she decided it was best he just glide out of her life. His kisses held the power to make her forget her goals. He was a dangerous man, one best left alone before he tore her life apart completely. Besides, she rationalized, she wasn't wife material for a man with his money and status. A man like him would want a confident woman who could help him in the corporate world. That certainly didn't describe her.

Then why was she so depressed? Darien pushed harder during her workout, taking out all her anger and disappointment on the treadmill, then punching bag. She wasn't aware of the strange smile her lips pressed into with each hit to the stuffed surface. In her mind she saw Vincent. While it started out as an exercise in release, it defeated her, his smile winning out over her aggression. She pulled off her gloves and headed to the shower. She kept remembering when he'd backed her up against the wall, dragging her over his hardness, feeling his heat.

It was after ten the next evening when her phone rang, and she thought to let the machine get it. The sketches in front of her were just about finished; she'd done enough for one night. The project had pulled together nice and quick. Her client was a busy woman who knew her tastes and her budget, an easy combination to work with. With a sigh, she reached for the phone on the fourth ring, just before the machine could pick up.

"Hello?"

"Darien, Vincent here. I'm sorry it's so late there, I didn't realize until I'd dialed..." His hesitation gave her a strange hope. Her adrenaline started pumping, her hand automatically going to smooth her hair back.

"Where are you?" she asked, afraid to start anywhere else.

"In Tokyo." His exasperated sigh enhanced his words.

"Oh."

"Yeah, oh. Not the first place I'd choose to be right now. Did I interrupt anything important?" She wondered if he was referring to a date or time with another man.

"No, just finishing up some work. How's business going?"

"Not good or I wouldn't be here at all."

"I'm sorry. Want to talk about it?" Darien pulled the elastic band from her hair and her headache instantly disappeared.

"Let's just say I didn't fly halfway across the world to be a referee. That's what I've been doing since I landed."

"What would you rather be doing?" His hearty laugh warmed her. She could picture his face, his cynical smile. She'd tried to stay with safe topics but realized her question could be interpreted in different ways. "Well, at least I made you laugh."

"Actually, you've been driving me crazy the whole time."

"I'm halfway across the world. How am I doing that?" Her voice dropped as she sat forward, took a pencil in hand and pulled a clean sheet of paper before her. While they talked, she sketched. "Vincent?"

"Darien, ever since I saw you walk into that auction, my calm and orderly life has dissipated before me."

"And that's my fault how? For going to the auction?"

"Yes. If I blame you, I don't have to take responsibility."

"I see, so that's how it's going to be." Darien laughed as she added several darker lines to her drawing, his eyes staring up at her. "Vincent, why are you having such a bad time?"

"I'm bored with it, Darien. All of it—the negotiations, the acquisitions. The whole process is rote now."

"And somehow I've done that?" She held back her laugh, somehow feeling better that he wasn't enjoying his time away from her.

"Absolutely."

"So tell me what's changed. Let's see if we can change it back for you."

"There's no going back, Darien. Only forward, and we both know it."

"That almost sounds like a dare," she whispered back.

"I know. I don't want you as an adversary, but anything else right now and..."

"And what, Vincent? Why do I have to be anything to you at all? You have a new perspective on the house. Other than that I don't see anything keeping us—"

67

"Don't start lying to me. At least when we're alone let's give each other the respect we deserve and not start lying."

"All right. You're attracted to me and I'm attracted back. We can act on it or not. At this point I'm leaning toward my initial reaction to you. I knew that first night you'd be trouble if I let you. Just because we'd be good in bed together doesn't mean we have to act on it. It would probably be for the best. You can get back to work and so can I."

"Feel better now you got that off your chest?" He laughed and she pictured his smug smile.

"Don't laugh at me, Vincent Leighton. I told you the first night I didn't want anything to do with you."

"Yes, you did. But it hasn't worked out that way and, to be honest, I didn't want to let you walk away. We're both stuck. We're both invested in this relationship, Darien. You couldn't have kissed me the other night the way you did if you weren't."

"Damn you, Vincent. Just leave me alone. In time you'll meet someone else or call an old girlfriend. I won't sleep with you for your convenience or mine!"

"No, never for convenience. For emotional need and release, yes, but never just to appease me. I'd be disappointed if you did. I expect you to keep your opinions and your values, even if they do make my life harder."

"Vincent, I'm so confused. What do you want from me?"

"Everything, Darien. But I know it's too soon to ask. You don't trust me yet, and that's your right. While it annoys me to distraction, it's still your right."

"And it would be my right to ask you not to call again."

"But you won't. Even though you don't want to

admit it to yourself, and especially to me, we're different together. There's more than chemistry or hormones at work here and we both know it. Hell, Darien, the night outside the auction house we both felt it. There was electricity in the air around us."

"Recognizing it doesn't mean I have to act on it." He laughed again and it grated on her nerves. Changing her approach, she let a smile slide onto her lips, one that matched his cynical smile inch for inch. Her voice became husky low and she wished she could see his face. "Vincent, you really know nothing about me. About my past."

"Someday you'll get around to telling me what's important."

"What *I* see as important *you* might not, and vice versa."

"Then we'll just have to spend the next years figuring out what's important to us."

"And what about what the rest of the world thinks?"

"As long as they're not in bed with us, I don't care what they think."

"That's an easy out and you know it."

"Yeah, but it's getting you all riled up, isn't it?" He waited through Darien's long silence before she finally accepted his perspective and laughed aloud. "That's why I called tonight. I needed to hear you laugh."

"If that's all you wanted, you should have said it right up front."

"Wouldn't have been the same. I had to earn it."

"Vincent, you confuse me at every turn." She heard the exasperation in her voice and she could picture his brown eyes. Feeling a low twinge, she knew his intentions were right. Somehow they were meant for each other, in this time and space, but Darien wasn't a woman who toyed with men. Instinct told her he was right and it made her want him more.

"I can relate. I should get back to the meeting. Darien, can I call you again?"

"Tonight?"

"No, but maybe tomorrow, depending on what happens here."

"I'll be out in the evening. Call me after ten."
Dead silence fell between them.

"You know I want to ask and won't. Did you offer that information to make me crazy, wondering how you'll be spending your evening tomorrow? And with whom?"

"No, but it is an added bonus I hadn't thought about."

"Now that's the Darien I'm falling in love with."
Voices could be heard in the background. "I've got to go. Until tomorrow night?"

"Yes, Vincent, tomorrow night."

"Night, Darien."

"Good luck with your meeting."

She held the telephone in her hand long after he'd hung up, his words swimming inside her head, "Now that's the Darien I'm falling in love with..."

****

His evening calls became habit. Her phone rang between ten and eleven each night he was away. Each night they verbally sparred over life and love, though not their own, just love in general. It was enlightening to say the least. She learned he was raised by his grandmother and he learned her father taught chemistry at a university just outside Chicago. She learned he hated pistachio in any form and he learned that while it gave her a headache, chocolate was one of her weaknesses. Each night they delved a little deeper, found out a little more about each other, stripped another layer away.

Each night she fell into a blissful sleep after his call. Just when she began to count on him, his calls ended. The first night he missed she figured he was tied up in meetings. After all, they were dealing with a major time difference, she justified. The second night she began to wonder if he was all right, if he'd been in an accident or...

The third evening she forced herself to leave the apartment. Darien went to a movie and ate popcorn and diet soda for supper. Once home she was still antsy and now annoyed with herself. After a long bath she pulled on an old work shirt and wound up in the studio, working on a final sketch for the restaurant in Soho.

She'd put on the *Déjà vu* disc of Crosby, Stills, Nash and Young for background and was gathering debris from her workspace when there was a loud knock on her door. For a second she didn't acknowledge it, then it happened again, louder. She hadn't buzzed anyone in the front door and she was instantly on alert.

Through the peephole she saw him, an arm balanced on either side of her doorframe. He was rumpled, with dark circles under his eyes. He lifted his fist to knock again, but she opened the door just in time to stop him, which threw him slightly off-balance.

"What are you doing here, and how did you get in?" Her voice was accusatory. Vincent shook his head before pushing past her into the apartment. She closed the door hard, turning as she spoke. "Vincent, why are you here and..." Whatever else she might have said was swallowed by his lips locking over hers, his tongue delving deeply into her mouth. She didn't pull away; instead, she took what he offered. His arms held her tight against him as hers found their way over his, locking behind his neck. He rested his forehead against hers when he pulled away. His eyes were closed, but his lips curved into a lazy smile.

"Does the music have to be so loud?"

She started to protest, then took a closer look at him, at the shadows on his face and the heavy lids of his eyes. Pulling from his grasp, she moved quickly and shut off the music. He stayed in the hallway as she detoured to the master bath. She glanced at her appearance as she took a bottle of aspirin from the cabinet. Her hair was still damp and her face scrubbed clean. She wore only the oversized work shirt and a pair of cotton bikinis underneath. She dismissed the impulse to change when she remembered the aspirin in her hand. After she grabbed a bottle of water from the refrigerator, she met him back in the hall.

He'd turned and was now leaning on the wall for support, his eyes closed, his right hand rubbing his temples.

"Here, take these..." He slowly opened his eyes and saw what she offered, accepting them gratefully, drinking the water to push them down. "Come inside," she started. Vincent shook his head and pushed from the wall.

"No, I'm not staying. I just want to..." He didn't finish his statement; instead his hand went around the back of her head and pulled her to him. In bare feet she had to lean up on her toes to accept his kiss.

"Stay here," she told him.

"No. My driver's waiting. I'm exhausted and I don't even know what time it is. I just wanted to see you, make sure you were real."

"I'm as real as you are, Vincent."

"Have dinner with me tomorrow night. I'll be back to normal then."

"I can't. I have plans." She held his eye and was sorry she really did have the opening to go to. The idea of blowing it off chased through her mind several times, but she didn't offer to cancel. She countered with another offer. "I'm free Sunday."

"All right, Sunday. I'll pick you up around noon." His fingers threaded through her hair, keeping her close.

"Vincent, you're dead on your feet. Either come in and lie down or go home to bed and get some sleep."

"Darien, if I come in I won't sleep and I won't do justice to you or me right now. I'm going home and apparently I'm not going to see you until Sunday."

"What would you like to do?"

"I don't have a clue. Dress comfortable and I'll figure something out." His fingers laced through her long hair one last time and he gently tugged her back a second time. "Is there another man, Darien?" His brown eyes held hers.

"No, Vincent. If there was, you wouldn't be here." She turned away, annoyed when he smiled. "Oh..." She shook her head in disgust at him and herself.

Carefully she moved around him and unlocked the hallway door, easing it open, his cue to leave. He moved quietly toward the outer hallway, pausing only to run his thumb along her cheek and down along her chin. He let the tip of it tease her bottom lip before taking a deep breath and pulling away. Darien stared as he fought back his smile once more.

"Sunday, Darien." He turned away.

She shut the door loudly after him and he finally laughed aloud. He'd known showing up at her place unannounced after almost three days of no contact would annoy her. He'd done it for himself. He did want to kiss her; that was his main reason. The other was just to make sure. While he'd been away, she'd kept plans but never elaborated much about them. His ego wouldn't wait any longer to make sure there wasn't another man.

Her anger when he asked had sealed her fate. And his, he knew. Forcing himself not to fall asleep in the car on the way across town, he was glad to be home, at least glad to be back in Manhattan. Especially now he'd found Darien across town. Moving mechanically through his apartment, he started to pick up the pile of mail his housekeeper had stacked, and then tossed it aside. Grabbing a beer from the kitchen, he downed it on the way to the shower. With just a towel wrapped around his waist, he padded toward the kitchen to review his food choices. Nothing appealed to him.

A wave of tiredness overtook him. He'd collapse soon. Vincent turned off the interior lights on his way toward the bedroom, pausing when he saw her scarf still draped over the back of the chair. On impulse, he pulled the silk to his fingers, then toward his face. It still carried her spicy scent. Keeping it in his hand while he settled on the large bed, the remote control for the television in the other, he decided on an all-news channel. His hand came toward his face once again, leaving the silk where he could inhale its fragrance, remembering how she looked, how the shirt barely covered her thighs. He'd watched her move away to turn down the music, taking in the sight of her long bare legs, the light revealing her body through the cloth.

He was head over heels in love with Darien M. West. Now he just had to figure out how to make her fall as hard as he had.

****

Saturday night came and went without much fanfare. The opening of her friend Otto's show was fun, but Darien began to feel restless soon after arriving. She knew she had to stay for a while; Otto had helped her out with some dynamic faux finishes in the last few years. Tonight was about him and his art, not her boredom and the fact she could have been with Vincent. Darien put on her social smile and said all the right things to all the right people until she could slip away. Finally at home, she toed off her heels and hit the answering machine as she passed.

"Darien, it's Vincent. I'll pick you up at noon tomorrow. Dress casual but warm. I thought we'd take a drive upstate."

The message ended, no good-bye or I miss you, just the facts. He was definitely a man with a minimum of words wasted. Soaking in the tub was the only thing she could think of to calm herself. The idea of seeing him tomorrow was too far away and she wished she had the nerve to do something crazy, like show up at his apartment this late, wearing only her coat. She laughed at the image and shelved the idea. Surprising herself, she slept easily and woke refreshed, without the usual case of nerves thinking of him usually brought.

Chapter Six

"Get your act together, girl," Darien whispered aloud to nobody but herself, suddenly anxious about her day. She was dressed and waiting in front of her building. She'd thought long and hard last night and was ultimately afraid they wouldn't leave her apartment if he came inside to collect her. It would be her choice. It was that fact that frightened her most.

Vincent seemed surprised, but didn't question her motives as she slipped into the passenger seat with a smile.

"Where are we heading?" she asked as she settled in and adjusted the seat belt. She gave him one sidelong glance as he pulled into traffic. His hiking boots were broken in as was the denim covering his strong legs. He had a white fisherman's knit sweater layered over a light blue denim shirt. All in all, she decided, quite a package.

"Upstate, if that's all right with you. I just wanted to drive for a while."

"All right, but why upstate, and not out to Long Island?" Her voice teased him, yet she wanted an answer. He gave her a sidelong glance, but she didn't push for an answer until he was through the worst of the city traffic.

Darien wondered how he'd be with her today. She knew he'd left his message just after eight, knowing she probably wouldn't be there. Now, sitting beside him, she relaxed. She wore a multicolored knit sweater over a white turtleneck. Her jeans and boots were comfortable.

"Vincent, why not Long Island?"

"There are other places..." He turned off the radio so they could talk. "I figured it would be easier if we stayed on neutral ground." The hint of a smile broke through and he didn't try to conceal it, she noted. "And as to why we're driving, it's simple. If we weren't, I'd be touching you and I know you're not comfortable with that yet. Am I wrong?"

"It's not the touching I'm uncomfortable with. It's where it will lead us that makes me apprehensive."

He snorted out another laugh. "Apprehensive? Is that what I make you feel, Darien?"

"Absolutely. You're like Pandora's Box, Vincent. Something I want, yet I know the minute I open it, it will change me. And I'm not sure I'm ready or willing to be changed...just yet."

"But you're thinking about it?"

"Yes." She turned to look out the window, watching the tree-lined parkway speed past her. "Vincent, please change the subject for a while, all right?"

"All right." A few minutes passed before he finally spoke again. "Were you born in Connecticut? Is that why your parents named you Darien?" He wasn't prepared for the outright laughter he got in response. It took him by surprise, especially when she laughed so hard she let a few loose tears escape down her cheek. After pulling a tissue from her purse, she blotted and tried to regain her composure.

"Oh, Vincent. See, this is just what I was trying to tell you on the phone last week. We really know nothing about each other. I was named Darien because that's where I was conceived. My parents were hippies, flower children. They had no qualms tagging me with a name that spoke volumes about their private life. I suppose my parents were some of the last holdouts, communal living and all that went with it." She shifted to see him better. "Does it embarrass you, or should I say, will it embarrass you when some VIP finds out? And before you ask, somehow they always do, even when I go out of my way to gloss over it."

"I don't care what people think in general, Darien. As long as I'm not doing anything that directly hurts or causes pain to a person, I don't care what they think about me. If it's business related, I care even less. I've never been a man who got hung up on labels. If I was, I'd be a different person."

He stopped talking when the traffic snarled and only continued when he passed the tie-up. "Leighton is my mother's family name. I told you I was raised by my grandmother. My mother was a child of the sixties too; so I know all about flower power and peace and, especially, free love." He paused and cleared his throat before going on. "She never knew who my father was, just a face she was attracted to after a party one night. I was born in sixty-eight and she left me with her mother soon after. She had a life to live and a child didn't make it any easier."

"I'm sorry, Vincent. But you're awfully well-adjusted for your upbringing."

"Grandmother saw to that. She gave me a stable home environment which I thrived in. I'll always be grateful for that."

"And your mother? Is she still out there, somewhere?"

"No, she died when I was seven. A bad hit of acid."

"Oh."

"So the origin of your name really doesn't bother me." His glancing look dared her to challenge him further.

"Would it bother you to know I posed for a men's magazine when I was in college?" She seemed to be waiting for his outraged reaction. Instead, he calmly changed lanes and took the next exit. Only when they were on a secondary road did he smile.

"*Playboy*, the fall issue. 'Girls of the Northeast Conference.'"

"You've known for how long?"

"Since the day we came back from Millner's. After I dropped you off, I did some research." He hesitated and then added, "No, that's not right. Lyle told me you'd been in print. I researched because of his information. Actually, I was quite impressed. Did you do it for the money or to piss off your parents?"

"Neither. I was a junior in college and had finally grown into my body. The offer came and my parents were very excited about it. Nudity wasn't an issue in our home when I was growing up. I did it because I was sick of being pigeonholed as a geek."

"You? A bookworm maybe, but never a geek."

"Well, not since then, anyway. It was my way of breaking out of my shell. I'm not sorry I did it. Body wise, I've never looked better than in that photo and it gave me more confidence than you might be able to understand."

"It doesn't matter to me, but you probably should tell me how you want it handled if it comes up in public and we're together. Personally, I'd prefer to boast that you've chosen me and aren't I lucky. What's your take?"

"I generally acknowledge it. Lying would be pointless. Although, in all honesty, it's been years since anyone recognized me or associated me with the layout. It's pretty much a done deal, but I wanted you to know, in case it embarrassed you."

"You, embarrass me? Never, honey. The only time I'm self-conscious is when my body overrides my good sense and leaves me erect while in public with you. And that's more of a personal comfort issue than a public one." This time it was Darien who laughed.

"All right, one more family confession, and then you'll know all my secrets." He only glanced toward her and waited for her to continue. "Will it bother you that my parents never married? I mean they've been together for, God"—she pushed her hand through her hair—"almost thirty-three years now, but they never formally married. They'd made a commitment to each other and didn't feel a piece of paper solidified it."

"I'm not a man to cast stones, Darien."

"I just wanted you to have the facts, so you wouldn't be surprised if someone tried to use it against you or me one day." She let out a relieved sigh.

"Do you really believe in this day and age people would try to use your parents' marital status as a road block?"

"It doesn't bother me, Vincent. I just didn't want you to get caught unaware."

"Point of information noted, and filed for future reference if needed. What about you, Darien? Will you need that piece of paper to make your marriage legitimate?"

"Yes, I will. I'm nowhere as strong as my mother, or as confident. And we live in a different time; I don't want my children to be labeled."

They were quiet for a long time, Vincent following the road while Darien watched out the side window.

****

"We okay?" Vincent asked.

"Fine. But I have a question for you, if you don't mind?"

"Go ahead."

"I've never heard anyone call you Vince. Isn't it allowed?" She tried to hold back her laugh and ultimately wound up biting her bottom lip.

"They may try once, but I don't answer to it."

"Point of information noted and filed for future reference." Letting herself finally laugh, she relaxed in the seat beside him. "Where are we going?"

"Apple-picking. There's a farm close to here. I figured it was a reasonable destination and something we could do outside. I'm sick of boardrooms, hotel rooms, and airplanes. I wanted us to be outside."

"Works for me," she told him as she leaned forward, turning up the radio. She let her left hand rest on the back of his seat, her fingers combing through the back of his dark hair.

The rest of the day flew by. Darien couldn't remember a better day. Being outside with him in the fresh air, the slight chill of the day making her drift toward his body heat, she let all her preconceived notions go for the afternoon. Today she was just Darien West and he, Vincent Leighton.

She teased him a second time that she'd never heard anyone call him just Vince and the look he gave her back told her why. It was her laugh that defused the look, and he accepted her teasing with a slight blush. The fact she didn't let his blush go unnoticed had him pulling her to him in a bear hug, a hug that went from comic relief to intense in a short amount of time. The kiss that followed made her press against him, made her want things from him she knew would be trouble. Today she didn't care. Today she just *felt*.

****

Vincent had decided that he was in love with her while he was away in Tokyo. If he were honest with himself, he'd known it the first night outside the auction house. Hell, he'd known it the moment he laid eyes on her. Today just reinforced his convictions. She would be his, if he was able to wait for her to accept the concept. Something made her leery of a relationship with him; he wasn't sure if it was just him, or all men. Today, when she forgot to be cautious of him, she shone in the afternoon sunlight. Highlights from her sable mane of curls reflected all around her when the wind rustled past them.

Vincent found himself walking away when they turned down a different aisle and she started talking with a young child. His mother stood beside him, her belly overloaded with another baby. He was whining because he couldn't reach the fruit. After some discussion with his mother and then the child, he'd watched from the distance as Darien scooped the boy up in her arms and then lifted him high enough to pick the fruit. Their combined laughter hit his heart in a way he'd never expected. In that very moment he could see her with his child in her arms and knew there was no turning back.

Never before had Vincent wanted a woman for a wife. In actuality he'd walked, and in some cases run, away from any female who wanted to tangle him up long-term. Now he knew how they felt, for it was a complete reversal with him and Darien. He wanted a relationship while she was still leery of spending time with him. Smiling at the fates of life, he'd wandered back toward her when mother and son had moved away.

****

Over supper they were easy with each other, a sample of the way they could be together. They'd laughed and been serious a few times, ultimately finding a comfortable path.

"Tell me, Darien, what are you going to do with all those apples?" He held her eye for just seconds before laughing.

"This, coming from the man who just had to have another bushel!" Smiling, her guard down, she watched him as if seeing him for the first time. They both felt the shift; she withdrew. "I'm going to make some apple pies with my bushel. I don't have a clue what you'll do with the rest of them."

"What would it take for you to make pies from mine too?" His eyebrow arched with the challenge. "Supper at the finest restaurant in New York?"

"Nope." She shook her head and smiled. "More food on top of pie? I think not."

"Rubies, then? A necklace or bracelet?"

"No, rubies clash with my skin tone." She quieted for a moment, watching him over her coffee cup. "I'd be willing to share some of my pies with you, for repayment of a lovely day in the country. But the rest of them are still yours."

In the end she'd taken most of their haul and he knew there'd be pie in his future.

He summoned all his willpower to the surface when he brought her home that evening. What he wanted to do and what he knew as right were two very different things. He understood enough about her to know she would tell him when she was ready to accept more from him. It didn't stop him from kissing her senseless in the hallway of her apartment.

"Want some coffee?" she asked when he pulled away from her lips at one point.

"If I stay, it's not coffee I'll want, and we both know it." He felt her tense in his arms, and pulled her closer. "Relax, I'm not staying, I know you're not ready...but Darien, when you are, we're going to have such a great time." His lips skimmed over her chin and down toward her throat. Vincent pulled the neckline of her shirt aside, sucking a small patch of skin between his lips. Her sigh told him he was on the right track, as did his pounding erection. "Darien, I have to go or I'll want to stay..."

"I know," she whispered, the tremor in her voice audible.

"You're not ready for me yet, are you?" He

already knew the answer but needed her to say the words.

"No, Vincent." He forced himself to push away from her warmth. When he did, her hand came up to cup his chin. "Thank you for understanding," she continued, her thumb running over his chin. "How did you get this scar?" She rose up on her toes and let her tongue slide across the crescent shape over his eye. He visibly shook at her touch and she looked at him.

"Stupidity..." he started, and then stopped when she repeated her lick a second time.

"Rifle kick back on you?"

"Yeah, the scope caught me. I was distracted at the time. Not the best way to go hunting."

"Do you hunt often?"

Darien's voice had lowered, the husky tone made him think of sex, want, and need as her hands slid over his shoulders. "No, this was a conference on an estate in Montana. At the time it seemed harmless, until I realized I was about to kill something so small that had never done anything to me. I flinched to miss and the scope kicked back."

She rested her head against his chest. "I'm glad you missed, just for general principles. It's one thing to hunt for food, another just for sport."

"My feelings, too." His hands made lazy patterns on her back as she tucked her fingers into his back pockets. "Darien..." Vincent felt her heat against him, felt himself pulse, felt her accept his need and shift over him. It made him harder and she shifted again, the cycle beginning to make him change his mind and take her, there and then.

"I know you should go." She moved from his embrace and a visible shudder ran through her. "The thing is, Vincent, I've never wanted a man as much as I do you and that frightens me on several levels. Not the sex..."

"It's the intimacy factor that's got you scared."

"I suppose that's part of it. The other part is what will be left of me when you realize I'm not right for you?"

"That might not happen."

"And still, it might. I just wanted you to understand where I'm coming from. I'm not afraid of you physically; just emotionally."

"Point taken and I'm leaving before I screw up a wonderful day." He moved away and paused outside her door. "I almost forgot, next Saturday night I'm hosting a cocktail party at my apartment. Unfortunately it's business, but if you came it would brighten my evening." He gave her a smile that he hoped would melt her heart.

"I'm not sure what to say, actually. What does my being there say to your business associates?" She leaned against the door frame with her arms crossed over her chest.

"It says I have excellent taste in women. Think about it. I'll call you tomorrow night."

****

All through the day she pondered the pros and cons of going to his party. On one hand, she wanted to see him in his element. Her brief sojourn to his office had given her a glimpse of his professional life. On the other side, it would tie her to him publicly. Then there were the business contacts she might make and the repercussions of them being seen as a couple. It was all maddening. Darien realized she was making a big deal out of it when it was simply an invitation to a cocktail party. Why shouldn't she attend his party, as long as she didn't read too much into them having a future together?

His call came at the usual time, but his voice betrayed his state of mind. He was tense and tired.

"You've had a bad day," she started.

"It just got better." His tone relaxed while they

talked about nothing, and then he brought up the party. "Have you given it any thought?"

"Too much, actually. I suppose I want you to understand that if I attend, it says a lot to the world about us and..."

"Darien, talk to me. What is it?"

"I suppose I want... Damn it, Vincent, my appearance will tell the world about our relationship, but I want to know before the world does!" She wasn't prepared for his outright laughter. She bristled at the sound.

"Oh, Darien. I've been trying to be so careful with you, not push you into anything you weren't ready for, but in my mind, we're a done deal."

"Beyond sex, Vincent?"

"Especially beyond sex. We would have been there and done by now if that's all I wanted from you. I'm talking long-term, Darien, and if I was there with you I'd see your face just lost all color. Am I right?"

"Yes, damn you. How do you know me so well, yet we hardly know each other?"

"It just happens that way sometimes. Don't you believe in kindred spirits or soul mates?"

"I hadn't pegged you as a romantic, Vincent." Now she was more confused than before.

"Until I met you, I wasn't." He paused, and then added, "Think about it, don't make a decision now. If you decide you're uncomfortable, that's all right for now. It would be better if you decided to come, but I'll accept your decision."

"I wasn't looking for this to happen, especially now, Vincent. My career and life are just on track."

"Then, when?"

"I never pictured myself with a man like you." Her words were beyond accurate on many levels. "You keep telling me you want honesty above all, well, there's honest. I don't see myself as what you need."

"That's for me to decide. What you need to decide is if you're willing to take a chance with me, Darien. And I want that chance."

"How much does this have to do with the house?"

"Nothing. Stan is back on track working from your rough changes. As I explained, I went to you because you understood my vision better than I was able to explain it. The house will go forward, Darien, with or without you by my side."

"I want some time to think this through."

"Not a problem. I'm leaving in the morning for Seattle. I won't be back until Friday. Take the time I'm away and decide. I know what I want from you and it's going to be permanent once we start. I'd like to have you by my side Saturday night, most importantly just for me, forgetting what it says to the world. If you don't come, I'll understand, and I won't bother you anymore."

"That sounds like an ultimatum, Vincent."

"I suppose, if pushed, that's what it is. We're not kids anymore, we're both in our thirties with careers and lives. I want to blend our lives and share them. You have to decide what you want."

"All right, I'll think about it."

"I won't call you this week while I'm away. Hopefully I'll see you Saturday night." There was a pause where they could only hear the other's breathing.

"Good night, Darien."

"Goodbye, Vincent." Darien didn't like being treated as a business deal, and that was how this conversation had made her feel.

She hung up the telephone and went to the kitchen. She poured herself a glass of wine, took two aspirin and walked to the window seat. Staring down at the street, she tried to figure out if he could be her future. The question didn't seem to warrant an answer. She knew it already.

What struck her as more important was what she would wear and was she trying to impress just Vincent, or all of his business associates? Laughing at her own insecurities, she left the glass untouched and headed to the closet. As she fingered each dress or suit, she pictured herself walking into his apartment wearing it, all eyes turning to her. Nothing seemed right. Darien knew she was in deep trouble. All her life she'd prided herself on dressing for herself, not to impress anyone else. Now that was just what she was doing.

She let out a low groan at the thought of being in love with Vincent Leighton and finally dropped onto her bed. Closing her eyes, she remembered how he touched her, how he kissed her, and how he felt pressed against her. She rolled over with a groan and tugged the pillow under her head. Yes, she wanted him at any cost, and she would go to his party. Whatever happened after that she'd have to wait and see.

Chapter Seven

Harsh November winds used the New York streets like a maze, ignoring some and ravaging others. Thankfully, Vincent's apartment faced a nondestructive direction. She'd spent too much time on her hair to let the wind ruin the effect she was going for. And Darien had decided to go all out. This had been a long week spent thinking about all of tonight's ramifications: what she wanted for herself, her future, and what she wanted back from Vincent. It kept coming back to Vincent and being with him. Had he called her during the week she might have felt different. But he'd stuck to his word and left her alone. His acute absence made her realize how mundane her life had become. Everything would work out between them, eventually, and only if it was meant to be. Darien truly believed that. Tonight, she wanted him to be both proud and awed by her. The doorman of his building opened the taxi door and smiled.

"Good evening, Ms. West."

"Good evening," she returned, not surprised he'd remembered her from her last trip there. The smile he gave her inspired confidence. He held open the building door and she smiled in return. "Thank you."

"Enjoy the party," he told her before moving back to his post.

The elevator was waiting; she took it as a good sign. When she got off on Vincent's floor, she stopped at the mirror in the vestibule. It was a large gilt monstrosity with a floral arrangement sitting on a marble-topped table under it. Darien checked her appearance one last time, took a deep breath, and walked down the long corridor toward her future.

A young woman in black pants with a white, mandarin-collared jacket opened the door. In the entry, Darien relinquished the emerald green velvet cape that matched her dress. And what a dress. While searching for fixtures for a new project, she'd seen it in a small shop in Tribeca. When she tried it on, even the saleswoman had taken a step back. It was as if it had been made especially for her. The squared neckline was cut deep and flowed into long, tight sleeves. Its waist was fitted, then flared from her hips, landing just above her knees.

It was the perfect blend of sex and innocence she'd been looking for. With the right lingerie, only the tops of her breasts were presented for public sight, but it led the eye to look further and realize how much was really covered. She felt good in it. Now she hoped Vincent thought the same thing.

****

He spotted her as she entered the living room. Dark green velvet hugged every curve. Vincent moved away from his assistant Mark and was beside her in an instant. While he'd made his way across the room, he'd glanced at the other faces turned toward her. His chest puffed up with pride and he felt lighter than he had all week.

He'd spent a nonproductive week in Seattle, hating himself for giving her an ultimatum over the party during their last phone call. What was important was their being together. Vincent had picked up the phone each night to call her, then stopped himself. He said he'd give her the week and he had—one long, frustrating week.

Darien had pulled her hair up and off her face, and anchored it with rhinestone pins and clips. Several long curls were pulled forward, framing her face. Her make-up was heavier than he was used to seeing on her, the result an erotic aura of spicy female. Vincent was old enough and experienced enough to recognize the difference between woman and female.

His hand stretched out to her while he was still several steps away. Her smile made his week of dread disappear. If only he'd been able to read her mind; he wondered what she was thinking. Apparently she'd decided she wanted him as much as he wanted her.

"You're stunning," he whispered when he reached her side.

"Thank you." They stood together, ignoring the other people around them until a waiter paused beside them, offering glasses of champagne from his tray, which she declined. Several messages had been passed without a single word being spoken. The intensity between them was almost palpable.

"Let's get you something to drink that won't give you a headache."

He led her to the bar in the corner, where she accepted a glass of sparkling water. A hand slapped him on the back, and he reluctantly turned away from her. "Mike, good to see you, thanks for coming. How's business?"

Vincent saw that Mike was eyeing Darien, and she looked uncomfortable but she didn't interfere in their conversation. Finally, when he had no choice, Vincent made the introduction.

"Mike, I'd like you to meet Darien West," he said. Mike's leering look at her had Vincent positioning himself between them. The other man took his hint, but moved away a bit too slowly. Darien held back a smile, her bottom lip between her teeth.

Vincent leaned closer. "Don't bite your lip, let me." And he did, right there in front of all his guests. His mouth found hers, tugging her lip with his teeth before capturing her in a long-awaited kiss. When he pulled back, she kept his eye.

"An effective way of marking your territory," she whispered, her voice almost hesitant.

"I suppose you could view it as that. I saw it mainly as a chance to kiss you."

"Two things accomplished at once. No wonder you're such a productive business man! You multitask beautifully." She threw back her head, favoring him with one of her husky laughs.

"Darien…"

"Relax, Vincent. I wouldn't have come if I didn't realize we were already an item. And I'm not sorry. I just hope you aren't in the future."

"Never," he whispered before taking her hand and pulling her into the throng. "Anyone specific you'd like to meet?"

"You decide. It seems like an interesting group."

"They're mostly all business, Darien."

"Then you decide who it's important that I meet tonight." Her eyes flashed, giving him control, if only temporarily.

"Right about now they're all secondary to you." She favored him with another bright smile and Vincent loved her a little more, if that was possible. "Want to skip the rest of the party instead?" She rolled her eyes when he laughed. He saw her nipples bud under the tight bodice.

"We should probably stick it out for a while…"

"Darien…" he started, but they were interrupted, never getting back to that particular conversation.

****

Introductions were made and Darien tried to retain names with faces, but it all became a blur. After what seemed like an eternity, but had in reality only been two hours, she excused herself and went to his bedroom, taking a few minutes to herself to check her hair and makeup. Her biggest fear about tonight was that Vincent had changed his mind, or that, after not seeing or speaking for the week, he'd seem different to her. Now her fears were allayed. Her decision to attend had been right. As she started to go back to the party, the hall door opened and closed. Someone had entered and shut off the lights. Darien took a deep breath. Who had come to join her? Vincent leaned against the closed door, his back squarely blocking entrance to anyone else. His arms were folded over his chest, his legs shoulder-width apart. She moved tentatively into the room, relieved when she realized it was him.

"Vincent, you scared me. I didn't know who came in and shut out the lights."

"I wanted a moment alone with you. Thank you for the dress."

She closed the distance between them in several long strides, tossing her purse on the bed as she passed. Her hands reached to his head, angling his face toward her. He accepted her kiss and countered with a second. Only when his hands went to pull at her hair did she move away. "We'd better get back or we won't leave this room tonight." She laughed at him, her hand reaching to retrieve her purse. "Leave it," he told her.

"You just want an excuse to draw me back to your bedroom later."

He stopped in his tracks and turned, a mischievous smile on his lips. "Want to sneak out?"

"Leave your own party, Mr. Leighton?" She was surprised to see he was somewhat serious.

"The party is secondary to you, Darien. You're my priority from now on." His face was tense. She knew he was trying to tell her something that mattered. It was what she needed to hear, and wondered how he knew.

"Thank you, but I suppose since you're the host

we should tough it out."

"Darien... All right, later." He raised one eyebrow in a resigned look before slipping out the door. The last thing Vincent wanted to do was go back to the party, but Darien was right. He was the host and his hormone overload shouldn't taint his common sense.

Darien laughed at him, tucking the small purse under one of the pillows on the bed. She took one last look at herself and headed back into the noise and conversation. Inside she was excited and nervous at the same time. Knowing the next few hours would change her life one way or another didn't help to calm her. Neither did the sensual heat kissing him created inside her. In the past she was never nervous, but she'd never invested her emotions in those relationships. This time her heart was gone before she had a chance to warn it.

Back in the living room she recognized Mark standing to the side, near the windows, watching the party around him. With a fresh glass of water in her hand, Darien made her way to his corner. He smiled politely and started to fidget. She held back a smile when she realized he was trying to look anywhere but at her chest. He was young, probably six to eight years younger than she. She decided to take his shy response as a compliment, giving him points for not staring at the boss' new girlfriend.

"I wanted to apologize for rushing past you in the office. I was...annoyed with Vincent at the time, but I shouldn't have put you in an awkward situation. I'm sorry, Mark." She saw his face turn red and caught Vincent eyeing them from across the room.

"Thank you, but there doesn't seem to be any harm done." He stumbled on his words, assuring her it was all right.

"Have you worked with Vincent for a long time?"

She sipped from her glass and surveyed the crowded room.

"He hired me right out of college. I'm going to law school at night. He's helping me with the tuition, or I'd never be able to afford it."

"Did you always want to be a lawyer?" His answer was accompanied by vivid hand gestures and several animated facial expressions. Darien was laughing before she knew it. She finally understood what Vincent saw in the young man.

"When I graduate, he's promised to take me on."

"And in the meantime, he gets competent help, and you get experience inside the corporate world."

"Something like that. If it wasn't for Vincent, I'd probably never have gotten into law school, let alone been able to swing a full-time job along with it."

"Quite a guy...," she all but whispered.

"Yes, he believes in taking care of his own." Mark hesitated before adding, "He's changed in the last weeks."

"Is that good or bad?" she asked with a laugh.

"I suppose his outlook is different. His priorities have changed."

"Mark, is that good or bad?"

"You should probably ask him that, Ms. West."

"Don't go all 'Ms. West' on me now, not after all we've been through together." Darien tossed back her head and laughed with Mark. She nodded across the room to Vincent, realizing afterwards Mike stood behind them, eavesdropping on the conversation.

****

They sat across the Formica table from each other in the brightly lit diner. Its old-fashioned, stainless-steel exterior and large windows invited people into a haze of neon lights and cases filled with outrageous-looking desserts.

"That was quite a list of who's who tonight. I'm not sure I'll remember all the names with the correct faces."

"Don't worry about it. None of them really matter to us personally in the long run. Although I will bet they won't forget you. You turned quite a few heads tonight, my dear." He tried to hold back a smile but didn't quite manage.

"Isn't that what you expected from me?"

"Yes, I suppose so. And you definitely accomplished it with this dress."

"I'm glad you approve. I didn't dress for them, Vincent. I picked the dress for you."

"And I definitely appreciate it, Darien. You've had me semi-erect since I saw you standing in my doorway."

"Is that a problem, Mr. Leighton?"

"Most definitely, but it's the kind of problem I like. You're going to make me work overtime for you, aren't you, Darien?"

"Would you appreciate anything less?" she teased.

"No. I'd be disappointed."

After they finished plates of meatloaf and mashed potatoes, they relaxed over coffee. Darien had tucked her legs up beside her on the bench seat and was leaning on the table. Vincent had discarded his tie before they left his apartment; his jacket was folded over on the seat beside him. The sleeves of his starched white shirt were folded back.

"Ready for a confession?" he asked, watching her response.

"Oh, yes. Tell me." She realized he was serious and straightened in her seat.

"Tonight, just before you arrived, I was sure you had decided not to come. It was the worst time in my life that I can remember, besides my grandmother dying. It's how I felt inside."

"Vincent?" She didn't want to assume anything from his words, rather wanted him to elaborate.

"The thing is, I've fallen in love with you and there doesn't seem to be a thing I can do about it. Actually, I don't want to change it or you. It's just that when I looked up and saw you it was like the weight of the world being taken from my shoulders." They waited while the waitress refilled their cups and moved away.

"I didn't want to come tonight. But that was never really an option. I spent all week trying to talk myself out of coming, yet here I am."

"What did you tell yourself?"

"That you were no good for me. That in spite of the fact that you're charming and funny, you drive me crazy at times, and exasperate me at others. And, you were smart enough not to push me too hard. That was your saving grace, Vincent. You gave me the time and option to make my own decision about you."

"I'm glad you made this choice."

"So am I, although I'm scared spitless at the thought of a relationship with you. And ultimately, it doesn't matter. My heart overrode my common sense. Just like it did outside the auction that first night."

"I was blown away that first night. When you walked in, I just knew that somehow I had to meet you. When I saw you laughing with Lyle, I became incensed and I didn't even know your name. Yet it bothered me." He hesitated and sipped from his cup. "I watched Sissy walk down the aisle and figured all hell was about to break loose, and then she hugged you. You smiled with such brightness, such warmth and light. I wanted you to see me that way."

"That was relief, pure and simple. I hadn't seen her in almost two months and I was genuinely glad to see her again. Eight weeks earlier my greeting would have been very different. In all my professional years, all the people I've worked with, she is the one client I won't work with again. Especially now that I know Lyle clued you in to my photo."

"Did you tell him?"

"No, never. And I never mentioned it to Sissy. I'm not sure how he found out. And somehow I don't think he shared the information with her."

"No, I don't think he would either."

They shared a laugh over the protectiveness the woman showered on her husband. If it worked for them, who was she to question someone else's relationship? She and Vincent were having enough trouble with their own. Darien looked at Vincent and her heart fluttered. He was so damned handsome, dark and brooding, yet she was drawn to him.

"And then when I realized you were bidding against me for the bar, I almost couldn't believe it," he said with a shake of his head

"I couldn't believe I lost the bar, mainly because I knew I'd have to come up with something to replace it with. But it all worked out in the end."

"Yes, it has." He looked as though he was about to add something else, but didn't. Instead, he watched her closely, his brown eyes penetrating. "Darien, let's get out of here."

"All right." She gathered her purse and waited while he lifted the long cape around her shoulders. He retrieved his suit jacket and his overcoat.

"Where to?" he questioned her, once they were outside the diner.

"How about your place? The caterer should be gone by now." There was no further discussion. He stepped forward to hail a taxi, but she put her hand on his arm. "It's only a few blocks. Let's walk." She helped him slide into his heavy coat, and then let him tuck her against his body for warmth. The crisp night had lost its wind and given way to a clear sky, dotted with twinkling stars.

"Darien, are you sure? Because once I have you, there'll be no turning back."

"I'm not sure of anything since I met you, but I do want you and I truly think you really care about me." His arm tightened around her shoulder once again as they turned the corner of his block. He was quiet while they rode the elevator up and relieved when they entered the apartment. Mark and the caterer were gathering up coats and gloves in the entry.

"Everything handled?" he asked Mark.

"All taken care of. If there's nothing else, I'll see you on Monday." Vincent helped Darien off with her cape and thanked the caterer while he hung up his coat. By the time both of them were gone, he found Darien on the balcony, staring up at the sky.

"What would you like?" His hands slid up and down her upper arms, moving her closer to his chest.

"I want you, Vincent," she told him as she turned in his arms. Her hands found his face and angled it toward hers. Then she pulled back from their kiss and reached for his hand. "Take me inside. I don't care what happens or how, I just want to be close to you."

He followed her inside, pausing only to shut the balcony doors. "I was about to offer you a drink, but I don't want to give you a headache."

"Got any juice?" She had her back to him, studying his CD collection.

When he returned they exchanged her glass of orange juice for the Miles Davis CD she held. He moved to the equipment with a sure hand, shaking his head at her choice of background. *Kind Of Blue.* How had she known it was one of his favorites?

She sipped from her glass and moved easily in the space, shutting off lights and finally going to his side. "Vincent, what do you want, and how do you want it?" His smile told her everything she needed to know. When he brought her closer, she expected he would kiss her. Instead he turned her around and started removing the pins from her hair. When it was finally down, his fingers massaged her scalp, dropping the curls around her shoulders. Only then did he shift her in his arms to give her the kiss she'd waited for all week.

The kiss was deep and mystical. Vincent stepped back to study her face before going back to take another. Darien drew away from him, reaching for his hand, directing him toward the sofa, where she dropped down beside him. They touched and explored through the entire length of the disc. When it ended and automatically started again, Darien realized she'd never wanted a man like she wanted Vincent Leighton.

His touch warmed her, his kiss excited her, and his hands on her drove her into a heightened state she hadn't known existed. She lay half under him, half beside him as his hand skimmed her thigh, his other hand angling her head toward his lips. It was a heady feeling she didn't want to lose. Darien knew from his hardened length pressing against her that it was up to her to take them to the next step. With a small sigh she pulled away from him. Startled at first, he stared as she stood and turned her back to him.

"Vincent, undo this please..." His hand shook as it slowly inched the long zipper down the length of her back. The dress parted easily from her shoulders and bared her back. She stepped forward, tugging the tight sleeves down her arms. When she was free, the dress dropped to the floor at her feet, a puddle of green velvet.

Vincent didn't hold back his gasp when she turned. Her strapless bra and bikini panties were a deep black. Her nude stockings were held up without garters, only lace at her thighs. The four-inch dark green suede pumps she'd worn gave her the illusion that had his mouth turning dry. Her smile made his heart skip. It told him she knew exactly how she looked and had dressed for him. Watching her move away, he saw she had retrieved her purse and taken out several small envelopes of protection, tossing them on the coffee table.

Her hands didn't shake as she slowly unbuttoned his shirt, the time it took driving him crazy. While he wanted to strip and drop her to the floor, he knew he wouldn't. Instead, he steeled himself for her assault on his senses. Her buffed nails pushed the cloth from his shoulder, dragging against his skin in the process. It sent a chill down his spine. Her lips found the cleft of his throat, the back of his neck, the soft spot behind his ear.

Every time he reached to touch her, she moved away. Taking her nonverbal hint, he tried to steady himself. It was an exercise in futility when her hot mouth found his flat nipple. Her teeth teased him and his erection throbbed against the material of his clothing. Darien didn't let up; instead she seemed energized by his reaction. Again her nails stroked his bare chest, her fingers tangled in the mat of small, dark curling hairs that traced a path to his aching sex.

Her fingers grazed his stomach lightly when she reached for his belt. His swift intake of air brought a smile to her lips and she pulled back to kiss him deeply. As she did, her hand found him, hard and waiting. Her palm stroked him through the layers of cloth, felt him surge in her hand. Dropping to her knees before him, she lightly pushed him down on the sofa. Darien watched him while she pulled off his shoes and socks, and then tossed them to the side carelessly. Only then did she reach for him again, urging him from his seat. This time she finished pulling his belt from its loops and tossed it aside as well.

"Darien..." His hands rubbed her shoulders and she looked up. "Are you sure?" was all he could manage.

"God help us both, Vincent, yes."

He didn't question her again, rather closed his eyes and let her take him. His mind tried to control his throbbing as her fingers worked the zipper of his pants. He was surprised when she stopped and took several things from his pockets. The money and wallet fell to the side table. That was when she used her hands to tug his pants and silk boxers down his legs in one smooth motion. He drew a breath as he bounced to life after his confinement. Her breath was warm against him, her hands and nails all over him. When she moved to take him in her hand, he sighed.

Vincent tried not to tremble as she studied him, acquainted herself with him. He succeeded until he felt the tip of her tongue run along his tender underside. His hands found her shoulders for support, and he needed it desperately after she engulfed him in her hot mouth. Time slipped away as she tasted and explored him. Vincent couldn't remember a time when he'd been so aroused. He'd had fun in the past with women and enjoyed them fully, but Darien was different. She was spiritual in the way she loved him.

When he was nearing the edge, he withdrew from her, dragging her up along his body and capturing her mouth under his. Her hands splayed on his chest as his hands pulled her bottom tighter to his ache.

"Damn it, Darien, you make me want to lose control..." His lips found her throat and played there.

"Then let go, Vincent."

"Later. First I want to touch." He reluctantly moved her back a step from him and turned her around. His hands reached from behind to hold her breasts. Her head dropped back against his shoulder, allowing him to fondle her while his mouth and lips played on her neck. Her hand unhooked the front clasp on her bra, freeing her breasts to his waiting fingers.

"Oh, Darien," he whispered as he felt the weight of her in his hands, kneading the flesh he'd dreamt about. His fingers tugged at her already taut nipples and she quaked against him. Her hand slid back between their bodies, capturing his interest, her movements timed with his. She groaned as he rolled her nipples between his fingers. He turned her around and suckled first one breast, then the other. Her hands went to his shoulders to brace herself, her head dropping back, her eyes closing.

Vincent dropped to his knees in front of her, his cheek pressed to the small swatch of black she was still covered with. He inhaled her scent mixed with her spicy perfume and knew he'd found the one thing his life had been missing: Darien. She fit him, made him crazy, and drove him too close to the edge to be good for his own needs. Yet each minute they spent together, he knew it was right. Throughout his whole life, he'd respected women and tried to be aware of their needs. Tonight, Darien had him on another level, in another world of what loving a person could be.

He was careful of his strength as his hands kneaded her buttocks and moved her closer. He slid the panties down her long legs and sighed when she was skin to cheek with him, a trimmed patch of brunette curls calling to him. Vincent went into overdrive, her body telling him what she wanted, and more importantly, what she needed, with every small move or shudder. When he felt her quake at his intimate kisses, he slowly lowered her to the floor. In the low light of the gas fireplace, she glowed under him. At first he thought to plunge deeply inside her, then hesitated.

"Vincent, please, I want to feel you..." Her hand stroked his shoulder and back as he leaned up to watch her. He couldn't hold back the smile, moving toward her breasts, his lips capturing her nipple just as his finger penetrated her moist warmth. Her body tightened around his finger and he knew he pushed her over a small cliff of release, and he couldn't wait any longer. He had the presence of mind to protect her, shifting only slightly before he was at her entrance. Vincent paused to take her face between his hands.

"Darien, look at me," he said as her eyes opened lazily. His cynical smile made her shake her head slightly. "God, Darien, I feel like I've waited all my life for you," he told her as he pushed inside her in one long, smooth stroke. For a second he was barred, but she shifted under him and accepted his full length with only a slight grimace. He felt her contract around him, and all rational thought was gone.

She moved her hips to take him deeper and his lips found hers. With long slow kisses he loved her until they built to a fevered pitch. Darien's fingers pinching at his hips made him hasten their movements, his strokes deepening with each push. And it was Darien who fell over the mountain he'd dragged her up, her body jolting under him and around him, like a vise on his erection. It was too much; Vincent let go of his restraint with one last push and a low groan.

Her hands teased at his shoulders and he started to move away but she held him.

"Darien, I'm too heavy."

"Stay anyway, just for a minute," she whispered as she flexed her inner muscles around him. He smiled into her chest, his head cradled between her breasts.

"Keep doing that and you'll have to accept the consequences," he told her as he felt himself coming back to life inside her.

"That was the plan..." she answered just before he took her breasts in his hands, pushing them together and laving his tongue over both nipples at the same time. When she contracted around him again, he rose up over her and took what he wanted. He realized that in the taking, she was giving him all of herself.

****

Vincent reluctantly moved from her inner warmth, exhausted and elated, aching from their position on the floor. Never had a woman taken him to the new places Darien explored with him. They managed to make it to his bedroom eventually and he finally stripped off her shoes and stockings before laying her across the bed. He stood beside it, staring at her in the night. The open curtains let in just enough light to see her, but wasn't harsh and glaring. He dropped one knee onto the bed beside her, coming to rest above her.

"Darien, you're perfect, simply perfect. I've never seen a more beautiful woman." His hand reached to stroke her breast and her nipple came to attention. "And oh, so responsive." He touched her other side and again she reacted. Her slight groan urged him on. "And you're mine, from now on, Darien. Understand?"

"Yes, Vincent, only yours," she uttered as his fingers teased her flesh. "Please, come back inside me."

"Not so fast this time. I want to enjoy you a little first."

"Two can play at that game, Mr. Leighton." Her hand reached to his fullness and cupped his growing interest.

****

In the middle of the night Vincent pulled her against his chest, his arms just short of being too tired to hold her. He brushed the damp strands of hair from her face and smiled.

"I know it's strange, but somehow when we met outside the auction I knew this would happen." Her fingers stoked his chest.

"I knew I wanted you the moment I saw you in that green dress. Most of all I knew I wanted to take you out of it."

"I suppose that could be arranged. Tell me when and I'll wear it again for you."

"Darien, you're going to drive me insane for the rest of my days, aren't you?"

"That long?"

"At least that long." He pulled her closer, liking her body against his. Exhaustion and emotion had finally caught up with them.

"Vincent, can I ask you a question? An indelicate one to say the least?"

"Ask me anything. I'll answer you if I can." His fingers stroked her arm and held her tight.

"I'm not up on current protocol. Am I supposed to stay or go home?"

"Stay, Darien. Are you comfortable?" was all he had to say.

She relaxed beside him. A verbal answer was unnecessary. Vincent knew at that moment all his hints about the rest of his days had been accurate. He didn't want her to leave him, ever. And he was smart enough to know he'd have to give her time to see his perspective.

She shifted against him in her lazy state, her leg dropping over his. He was exhausted and had never felt better. He realized for the first time in his life he was content. Hours later he moved from beside her, pausing to pull up the blanket over her. She looked so peaceful in her sleep, her hair spread across his pillows. The whole room took on the scent of her perfume and their loving.

He moved through the room quietly, so as not to wake her, pulling on a pair of pajama pants made from dark blue silk. In the kitchen he drank down a bottle of water, then a second before going to his stash drawer. From it he pulled a box of English cigarettes and a silver lighter before moving to the balcony. He was just lighting a second cigarette when he noticed a change in the light behind him. Darien stood in the doorway, her shoulder resting against the frame.

"Was it so bad to be with me you resorted to smoking?" Her voice was still heavy with sleep when she encircled his waist from behind.

"You know better than that, Darien. This is one of my vices. Do you mind?"

"Depends," she told him dreamily as her hand ran along his bare chest.

"On what?"

"Whether you're going to share with me or not." Vincent slipped his arm behind her and pulled her in front of him, enveloping her against his body. When she was settled with her back against him, he passed her the lit cigarette.

"Fair warning. They're pretty stale." She drew on it deeply and didn't choke. His lips curled into a slight smile and his original thoughts of her being perfect for him were reinforced. She took a second puff before handing it back.

"It still tastes wonderful. I was a Marlboro Light girl myself."

"The soft stuff. I started on Camels and eased down to Pall Malls."

"What made you stop?" she questioned.

"Peer pressure mostly. I couldn't smoke in some places, meetings and such. It got easier to quit than want one and not have it. Now I save them for special occasions."

"And really bad days, I suppose," she teased. His arms tightened around her and he put the tube to her lips, waiting while she drew on it.

"No, never a bad day. It would be too easy in a down state of mind to get hooked again. And never indoors—it would be too simple. I only let myself have one or two to celebrate milestones."

"Turning me into a milestone, are you?"

"Elevating is more like it, Darien."

They were quiet while they shared the rest of the cigarette. His chin rested on the top of her head lightly.

"I hope you don't mind. I borrowed your robe. I couldn't seem to find any of my clothes when I woke up."

"And I was gone when you woke and you didn't know what to think?"

"Something like that," she admitted.

"I got up for a glass of water and couldn't resist. You okay?"

"Better than okay. I'm...wonderfully relaxed, except..." She felt him tense behind her and didn't hold back the smile he couldn't see.

"Except what?"

"Except that I want you again." Vincent understood how difficult the words were for her to speak and smiled into her hair. With a deep inhale he joked with her.

"You just want an excuse for another cigarette."

"Am I that transparent? Your bad luck, I'd say."

"My good luck, I'd say."

She turned in his arms and lifted her mouth to his tasting the mingling of tobacco and herself on his lips. It was a heady sensation when he realized he still tasted of her and he wanted her again. Persuading her wasn't a struggle. She seemed quite eager to get back inside and out of his bathrobe.

****

Darien woke the next morning in the sun-filled bedroom and knew exactly where she was. Vincent was sound asleep beside her. She allowed herself the luxury of watching him for several minutes before leaving his side, knowing she'd wake him if she didn't get up. Instead, she pulled on his robe and padded toward his kitchen, coffee the only thing on her mind.

That was how he found her shortly after—leaning on the counter in front of the dripping pot, her head cradled on her arms. He encircled her from behind. She went willingly against his body.

"I didn't mean to wake you."

"I smelled the coffee. Not a morning person, huh?" he teased.

"Not until my first cup."

"Darien, come back to bed with me for a few minutes. Then I'll bring you your coffee. I want you while you're still half asleep."

He watched as she looked to him and back to the pot, ultimately deciding on him.

Back in bed, the sheets a tangled mess under them, he took her quickly, using her languid state to mold her body under his. Neither of them was expecting the intense emotions that went with it. Only after she'd dropped her arms from around him did he roll to the side, his arm coming up to cover his eyes from the morning light. Neither of them spoke immediately.

Darien wouldn't have known what to say and was afraid "I love you" would gush out. Finally she managed to gather her wits.

"You promised me coffee."

"I did, didn't I? What would it cost me if you got it?"

"A very heavy price, Mr. Leighton. You'd have to

do me again!"

"A price I'm willing to pay, Darien. But since I promised, I'll go." He moved from beside her and she pulled the pillow under her head.

"Wake me when you get back." He laughed, and then disappeared from sight. Darien was glad to have a minute alone. She allowed herself the full grin of delight she'd been holding back. When he returned with a mug in each hand, she forced herself to sit up, pushing her hair from her face before accepting his offer. He slipped in beside her, a strange look on his face.

"What?" she asked, suddenly self-conscious about her appearance.

"Do you like to travel?"

"Most of the time. I'm not good for much after a major time change. It takes me a few days to get back on schedule."

"What are your plans for Thanksgiving?"

"Nothing very important. I've had a few offers for supper but haven't really thought much about it yet."

"I've rented a condo in Vermont. A little skiing and some downtime. Want to come with me for a long weekend?"

"Why, Mr. Leighton, what could we possibly find to do for a whole weekend together in a cabin in the woods?"

"I'll think of something to keep you entertained, Darien."

"I bet you will... Sounds promising," she said, leaning to put her coffee on the side table.

"Want a preview?"

Her hand went to his chin and drew him toward her. "Previews will have to wait. First you have to feed me."

He moved out of her reach but turned back to take her hand. "Come with me, Darien. First a hot shower, and then breakfast."

She laughed openly at him but joined him under the hot spray in the large glass-block shower in the master bath. Only after they'd used the soap to aid in a sensual massage, and while she was blow-drying her hair, did Darien start to feel uncomfortable. When she left the bathroom, Vincent had gathered her clothes and laid them on the bed for her.

"Want breakfast first or home to change and then food?" Somehow he understood her angst without her saying a word.

"Fresh clothes, unless you're going to put a tux on to eat?"

"Home first, then food. But, Darien, you standing there naked, fresh from the shower, is not going to get us out of this apartment." To prove his point, he moved his lips to her breast and latched on, his tongue swirling against her. When his motions stopped she slowly she became aware and drew a breath.

"Oh, all right. Food first," she conceded. "Then can I have an encore performance?" Darien dressed quickly, knowing he was watching her in the mirror over his bureau. She pulled on her panties and settled her large breasts in the black bra.

The same mirror afforded her a view of Vincent, watching his erection fill when she sat on the foot of his bed and pulled the stockings up over her smooth thighs, then stepped into her high heels. She wiggled into the dress and arranged it over her hips first, then her chest and arms, then moved toward him, stopping just inches before him, and turned her back. "Can you get this for me?" Her hand held her hair off her neck and he used the moment to scatter a line of light kisses along her spine before finally zipping the dress.

Chapter Eight

Darien enjoyed holidays when she was a child, but as an adult she usually wished the days over with. Unless she was at home with her parents, the holidays dragged for her. She had friends to share her time with, but they too were usually single and it just wasn't the same as being with her family. She knew she would go home for Christmas this year, so Thanksgiving hadn't seemed important. Just another weekend to get through. Now, on the drive back from Vermont, sitting beside Vincent, she knew what a holiday could really be like, if you spent it with the right person.

They'd left the city early Wednesday morning, Darien napping beside him for the first hours. When they arrived hours later, it was easy to wander through the condo with him. He dropped their bags in the large master suite, which was decorated in purple and white.

"Lavender isn't my favorite color," she teased, "but at least it isn't tan."

He'd rolled his eyes at her and continued to check out the accommodations. The master bath was luxurious to say the least, its double whirlpool calling to her after the long ride. They decided to settle in before getting sidetracked.

The main floor was basic. Living and dining rooms fronted the space with the kitchen at the rear. Fully equipped and fully stocked, she noted, right down to the juices she liked and the water she was always drinking. The upper level held four basic double guest rooms with two full baths. The lower level was a play space with a large wet bar area, a pool table, and several seating areas scattered around different game tables. Another surrounded the wood burning fireplace and yet another was designed around a huge television, hung on a back wall. Yet another bedroom and bath were tucked beside a steam sauna.

"I've died and gone to heaven for three days." She stood beside the open sauna door, surveying the space, liking the implications it granted. "Were you really going to come here all alone, in all this space?"

"Yes. I didn't see it that way, only as a place to get away to. And technically, I'm not alone." He lifted one eyebrow toward her as he pulled her to him. "Come upstairs. Let's get a fire started and take the chill off the place."

She went willingly.

****

The next days and nights were a haze of skiing, eating, and loving. Thanksgiving day he was up early to put a small turkey in the oven. Darien was promptly shooed from the kitchen several times during the day when she offered to help.

"This is supposed to be your weekend off, remember? I told you I'd take care of Thanksgiving."

"You're right. This will probably be the only time in our lives you'll take control of a holiday." He'd grabbed her in a bear hug against him, which led to several rounds of long kisses, exploring hands and minds.

"I like Thanksgiving. Let me have it." Vincent said more with his eyes than with his words.

"Which means I'm going to be responsible for all the rest of the yearly holidays?"

"Yeah, you probably are. But I promise to always give you Thanksgiving off."

"What a guy!" she started, realizing how husky her voice had become, how warm it was beside him with all the smells and mess of the holiday around them. "How much time do you have?" Darien's hand swept along his belly, dropping to cup his erection.

"The rest of our lives," Vincent had answered, seemingly unaware of what he'd said, adding quickly, "For now, we have another hour before I need to check the turkey. Want to try out the sauna or the bed?"

"The couch is closer, and you can still hear the game in the background," Darien told him, directing him toward a large overstuffed sofa, where she straddled his legs while she slowly unbuttoned his shirt. The football was forgotten, but the timer on the turkey roused them from their sleepy respite after their interlude on the couch.

"So, we have a deal? I'll do Thanksgiving, and you handle the rest?" he asked, buttoning his shirt as he moved toward the offending buzzing noise.

"I suppose it's the best deal I'm gonna get, so I'll take it." She felt no regret settling back on the sofa, the game still going, while she read through the various newspapers that appeared on their doorstep every morning.

In the early evening, sated from his surprisingly extensive feast, they dressed and wandered the woods with a light snow falling around them. She especially appreciated the fresh supply of firewood waiting in the rack just outside their door. Somehow they managed to deplete their stock each night.

****

On their last night there, they were lounging in the sauna when Darien brought up a subject she thought might be tricky. The episode had stayed with her and she knew it would until she talked to him about it.

"Vincent, I don't want to spoil our weekend, but I'd like to talk to you about something."

"What's wrong? What don't you like or want to

try again?"

She realized he thought it had something to do with them and smiled. "Wrong track. This isn't about us directly. It's just that last week, when I came to your place, I had a strange meeting." This time he sat up and took a towel to his face, wiping it before giving her his full attention.

"What happened?"

"It's nothing really. I rode up on the elevator to your place with a guy I met at your party. He didn't actually do or say anything in particular. I just got a creepy feeling about him."

"Who was it?"

Since she had his attention, she decided it was best to get it out in the open before she made a mistake she couldn't take back. "That guy, Mike. He was the one leering at me the night of your party." She watched him bristle beside her and reached for his hand. "Nothing happened, really. It's just that my first instinct was to let him know verbally I didn't like his attention, but then I wasn't sure who he was, and I hesitated. I didn't want to screw up business for you, but he did make me uncomfortable."

"Tell me exactly what happened."

Darien watched Vincent try to control his anger. "Really, it was nothing. We were in the elevator and I didn't think twice about it because for the first few floors there was another couple with us. When they got off, the vibe around us changed. He just gave me a creepy feeling. I can't explain it better than that. We didn't talk and he didn't actually do anything. It was just the way he looked at me." She paused for a breath and the right words to continue. "If I hadn't seen him at your party, I would have given him a dirty look and dismissed him. I guess what I'm trying to say is, I need to know, if I run into him again, how do you want me to handle him? Is he important to your business?"

"No, not at all. I only know him from the building. I already had Mark take him off all the guest lists. If he bothers you again, take him down, Darien. Verbally, or physically if you have to, understand?"

She nodded her understanding, and then smiled. "It would be easier to take another elevator."

"That too, but let me know if he bothers you again."

"All right, but don't misunderstand. He didn't say or do anything technically, just his attitude changed suddenly. I was uncomfortable. Don't worry. If I see him again, I'll make him sorry for his attitude." She hoped he realized she could take care of herself.

"I'd love to be a fly on the wall... I'll talk to him, see it doesn't happen again."

"No. Let it go. Now that I know he's not a business associate, I'll handle him."

"Yes, I'm sure you will." Vincent was learning not to override her decisions. Darien took it as a good sign that they were in sync.

"Besides, if you mention it, it will only feed his advances and stares. Let it go, all right? I just didn't want to drop one of your clients in the elevator and find out later it was a mistake."

"Drop him if you have to. He's nothing to me, but I'd rather you avoided him if possible."

"My sentiments exactly." She moved beside him, wiping his face before leaning forward. "Vincent, there are six bedrooms in this place and we've only explored one so far. Pick a room," she told him, then walked from the heat of the sauna. Outside the air felt cold and her nipples hardened on contact. Vincent was behind her, his hands reaching to her raspberry peaks, telling her the closest bed was his choice.

Days of skiing and exploring the area ended with them in each other's arms each night. His stamina surprised her, but she wasn't sorry. Instead, she accepted what he offered and gave him all she could.

****

Vincent pulled her to the side of the rest-stop convenience area as soon as she left the ladies' room. His whole persona had changed since their pit stop. "What's wrong?" were the first words out of her mouth when she saw the look on his face. He hustled her toward the truck, waiting until they were safely locked inside before turning.

"Darien, did you have a good time this weekend?" His brown eyes were darker than she'd ever seen before. The intensity alarmed her.

"Yes, Vincent. I had a wonderful time. Tell me what's happened to change it?"

"Nothing's changed between us, right?"

Confused, she nodded.

"Darien, you do know I've fallen in love with you. You do understand that?" She smiled through her fear and his eyes lightened.

"Yes, I think you do love me, and you know I wouldn't have been here with you if I hadn't fallen in love with you. Now tell me what happened in the time it took me to pee."

He laughed openly, pulling a folded newspaper from under his jacket. Slowly he unfolded the tabloid and handed it to her. The photo said it all—there was no need for the two-inch headline that read Bunny Bumps Financier. The picture had been taken through the diner window the night of his cocktail party. Darien stared at it and the particular pose that was chosen.

She was leaning on the table, her hand stretched halfway across it. Vincent's hand held hers and they were both laughing. The particular angle gave her credit for a larger bustline than she naturally sported. The article was all conjecture, mostly about Vincent, with only one paragraph about her. It said she was an architect and interior designer only after citing her *Playboy* photo shoot. The paper went on to speculate how she got her clients.

She could feel Vincent's eyes on her as she read. When she finished, she folded the paper and handed it back, hoping her face was blank as dread washed over her.

"It must have been a slow news week." When she didn't laugh, he said, "Darien, I don't have a problem with this, and I don't want you to, either." His hand came up and cupped her chin, drawing her toward him. "Darien, talk to me."

She took several deep breaths and did the one thing he probably hadn't expected. She threw open the truck door and bolted from its warmth, wandering along the grassy shoulder, her arms hugging her body. He let her go, leaning on the side of the vehicle while she worked it through. When she turned and realized he was still watching her, she moved quickly toward him.

"I'm sorry, Vincent." She hesitated to touch him. He pulled her to him with a little more strength than he ever used on her before.

"Darien, I don't care, and you have nothing to be sorry for. Besides, by next week some other couple will be caught having a night out and push us from the headlines."

"Are you sure? This won't hurt your reputation?" Finally, she looked him in the eye, wanting a truthful answer.

"My reputation isn't at stake over this. It's yours that could be tarnished."

"Mine?" She realized for the first time how the article was slanted and understood what made him so upset. When she first read it, she saw it as a hit to him personally. Apparently, he'd read it and saw it the other way around. "You're not upset?"

"Only because when I saw it I knew you would be." She looked at him for a long time before letting a smile break on her lips, her teeth automatically trying to pull it back.

He leaned down, whispering, "Let me, Darien," and sucked her bottom lip into his mouth with a now practiced ease. Vincent's actions sent a chill of heat down her spine. When he deepened the kiss she draped her arms around his neck, taking all she could from him. "We okay?" he asked when he drew away for air.

"Yes," she whispered, taking his mouth to hers for a second, then third, kiss.

The winds kicked up dust, and sand blew through the open parking area around them. Only then did he help her back inside the truck, pausing by her side before closing the door. He gave her one more heated kiss before adding, "That's got to last me all the way back to the city..." This time she laughed at him and he closed the door.

Miles later he handed her his cell phone. "Your parents will see it. Want to head off disaster?" He wasn't prepared for the shout of laughter he got in response.

"You forget who you're dealing with, Vincent. My mother will probably frame the article and dad will want to meet you."

"Would that be so bad?"

His words sobered her instantly and she answered slowly. The idea had crossed her mind several times during the weekend but she kept pushing it back. "Actually, no, it wouldn't. Want to come to Chicago with me for Christmas?" Darien gave him credit for staying in his lane at her question. He glanced at her quickly, and then turned his attention back to the road.

"If I could clear things at the office it might not be a problem. Can I get back to you in a week or so? I should know where I stand by then."

"Of course. It's weeks away. Let me know what you decide." Their conversation was automatically over as she reached for the radio. She turned it until she found a news station and lost herself in the world's problems. A short time later Vincent reached for her hand and drew it to his lips, dropping a small kiss on her palm.

"We're okay, Darien. We make the decisions. I've made mine. I want you in my life, all the time. One tabloid photo isn't going to change that."

"All right, Vincent. As long as it won't bother you that your 'bunny' girlfriend has a reputation for getting her clients the old-fashioned way!"

"Not a problem. Anyone who really knows us will know the truth, and anybody who speculates isn't worth our time." He dropped their hands to the console but didn't let go until he neared the city and traffic mounted.

****

Surprisingly, he found a parking spot across from her building, and it was easy to help her upstairs with her bag. As soon as they entered her apartment, he moved past her to drop her luggage in her bedroom. On his way out of the room he watched her hit the button on her answering machine. If he didn't know better, he'd have thought it was Darien's voice on the tape.

"Hello, sweetheart, it's your mother, but you knew that already. We saw the photo. Dad would like to meet this Vincent Leighton and have a talk with him. Me, I just want to see him in person and drool a little! Bring him home for Christmas if you can. I'll call you next week." There was a pause before the voice added, "Darien, don't let this get between you two. Somehow I get the impression he's right for you. Don't make any hasty decisions. Call me if you need me. Love you, bye." The machine clicked off and he watched as she let out the breath she'd been holding since it started. There were several other messages, but she paused the machine and turned.

"You know your parents well, Darien. That says a lot about all of you. I'll see what I can do about getting away for Christmas if it's still what you want."

"Of course it's what I want."

"Good, then let's scan the rest of these and be done with it." He moved beside her and hit the button, leaning against the wall as they laughed at the comments. The gambit ran from, "You go, girl!" to "Oh, you poor thing, imagine being painted as a harlot!" Vincent laughed at the term.

"Harlot? Who the hell was that?"

"Doesn't matter, Vincent. You were right. How we approach the situation will set the tone for anyone else. I'll laugh it off and drop it. Anyone who pushes isn't important."

"That's my Darien." He paused, laughing aloud, watching her bristle at first. "I'm only laughing because I thought you were crazy to have an old-fashioned answering machine instead of voicemail on your cell phone. Now I understand. The thing would have driven us crazy all weekend."

"A small way to keep my privacy, even if it is out of step," she admitted.

"Should I turn my cell back on? We can listen to my voicemail if you like?"

"Not now." She leaned up to kiss him, and then drew back with a strange smile. "Save yours for me to listen to later."

"Absolutely. I'll call you later and play them for you."

"You listened to them at the rest stop, didn't you?"

"No, I didn't. I saw the newspaper and was more worried about you than my voicemail."

She gave a small, all but nonexistent nod of her head, the one he'd come to know so well.

"I should go. We both have to get back to reality tomorrow morning."

"Vincent, I had a good time this weekend. Thank you for taking me away."

"Anytime, Darien." He hesitated before adding, "You going to be all right alone tonight? Want me to stay and scan your calls?"

"You can stay, but not to scan calls. If you stay it's to pleasure me!" The green of her eyes flashed golden and he knew she would be all right.

"On that note, I think I'll go home, crawl into bed, and get some sleep. I'll see you Tuesday night for supper."

"Absolutely." She walked him to the door and they both hesitated. Vincent finally spoke.

"I don't want to leave you, Darien. After this weekend, it feels wrong."

"I feel the same way," she told him.

"Call me tomorrow on the cell if anyone gives you any problems about the article, all right?" She muttered a yes that was swallowed up against his lips.

Vincent left half an hour later, both frustrated and content in a strange way. He'd all but asked her to move in with him but managed to hold back the conversation so as not to scare her. He accepted how much she valued her privacy; moving in with him after only a few weeks wasn't her style.

****

Just when life was settling into a comfortable routine, all hell broke loose. Over supper in a small Italian restaurant, Darien reached across the table for Vincent's hand. "Tell me what's wrong or I'll make up something myself."

Her smile melted away the bad day he'd had. How she managed to comfort him so consistently he'd never know. "Bad week at the office. I'm on overload and unfortunately I have to go away for a few days. I tried putting it off, but I can't."

"How long will you be gone?"

"Probably a week, but hopefully after that I'll be free for the holidays."

"Then go, take care of business, and come back so we can enjoy Christmas." She glanced at him. "Are you still coming to Chicago with me?"

"Yes, of course." His fingers tightened around hers.

"Are any of these problems related to the tabloid story?" For the first time since she'd met him, he hesitated. She slipped her hand from his and pushed back in her chair. "Anything we can do to dispel your problem?"

"No. Relax, Darien. I'm annoyed with having to go away, that's all. Before it was never a problem. I wasn't leaving anything important behind. Now the thought of being away from you for so long isn't appealing."

"Is that all, Vincent?"

"I promise. Everything is going to be fine. I'll take care of business and actually take a vacation over the holiday."

****

Darien always felt there was no other place like New York at the holidays. While it was crowded and cold, the atmosphere was charged with an undercurrent of hope. Detouring to head past the famous Lord & Taylor window display, they took their time viewing the winter wonderland scenes, becoming lost in the crowd around them.

Vincent hugged her tighter to his body, and she

moved easily with his intention. "Reminds me of Christmas with my Grandmother," he'd said, but his voice was so low she didn't know if she was meant to hear it, or if it was just for himself.

Darien didn't question him. Instead she directed him toward her apartment. In the warm confines of her space, she drew him to her bedroom and loved him with all her heart. Hours later, when he was getting ready to leave, she pushed up on her toes and placed a small kiss on the scar over his eye. "I'm going to miss you this week," she whispered, and his arms pulled her tighter. She held on as if she'd never see him again, something deep inside her making her wary of the situation.

"I'll call you tomorrow night."

"I'll be waiting," she told him with a good-bye kiss that didn't hint at his leaving, but more propositioned him to stay. He swung her legs up in his arm, carrying her back into the bedroom. He took her quickly, not bothering to undress, only to push his clothes out of the way. The long silk robe she'd covered her nakedness with to walk him out fell away with the tug of its belt, freeing her to him. Intense and erotic, she lay breathless under him, her hand holding his head to her breast.

"Damn it, Darien, why do I always lose control around you?" He sat back, taking the majority of his weight from her. Rolling on his side, his head propped on his hand, he used his free hand to run his finger down the length of her side, smiling when she stretched into his movements. "Oh, no," he laughed, and forced himself to get up. Back at the door they started a repeat performance. Vincent pulled back from her. "If I don't leave now...I don't want to go, but if I don't it will interfere with the holidays."

"Then go and finish, so you can come back to me."

"I'll call you..." He gave her one last kiss then turned back. "Want to come for a ride?" Her lips curled into a smile. "My driver has to come back to the city anyway."

"Give me five minutes..." She disappeared down the hallway, returning shortly in jeans and a white sweater that hugged her ample bustline and slim waist. She'd run a brush through her hair but hadn't put any makeup on. Tugging on a camel-hair overcoat as she walked toward him, she paused. "Vincent?"

"God, Darien," he reached for her hand and drew her to him. "It's a good thing the car has a privacy screen."

Finally settled beside him in the back of the warm car, she leaned forward to get rid of her coat, using his body for added warmth. "Did you push back your flight to have supper with me?" Her voice was low and husky, her perfume spice mixed with their recently loved bodies. There was no mistaking his straining erection against her leg as they left Manhattan.

"Would you feel better if I said yes?"

"Absolutely," she answered quickly, tucking closer to him.

"Then, yes. But I also figured I could get a few hours sleep before I get to the coast. And I'll have a few hours before the meeting to go over the changes."

"Thank you," her kiss elaborated on her feelings.

They were nearing the private air strip when he pulled her tighter. "What would you like for Christmas, Darien?"

She thought before she answered, not wanting to sound impulsive or needy.

"I'm getting what I truly want. I wanted you to come home with me and meet my family, and most of all I wanted us to spend the time together."

"You're an easy woman to please."

"On occasion, but I wouldn't get used to it if I were you."

"I'll keep that in mind."

"What's your best Christmas memory, Vincent?"

"I suppose being with my Grandmother when I was young. She always made a big deal of Christmas, decorating the house, baking cookies, the ritual of putting up a tree, writing the cards. Her favorite part was opening the cards each year. She'd tape them to every doorway in the house and each winter we'd touch up the moldings where the tape marred the paint. Don't get me wrong: at the time I thought it was a hassle and a waste of time, but she always managed to make the holiday feel like a holiday, not just another long weekend to get through before normal life resumed." He paused and drew a deep breath. "It was the tradition of it, Darien, not so much the presents, although they were good too. I was lucky to have her for as long as I did."

"I wish you still had her here with you, but you know she's with you in spirit."

"Can't change the past, Darien. Don't bother to try to influence the future." He pulled back from her and watched her closely for a long time. "Darien, you do know you're my future?"

"I hope so, Vincent." His kiss turned away any other thoughts as the car slowed to a halt. He stayed with her until his luggage was loaded and he had no choice but to leave her. Darien didn't get out, only left the car door open, watching him board the plane, pulling her coat around her shoulders and waving. He turned back one last time before boarding the plane. When he'd disappeared, the driver closed the door and drove back to the city. The whole drive home she thought about his words. By the time they reached her apartment she knew exactly what she

wanted to do and how to set about making it happen.
****

The week sped by. Darien had too much work to do and she wanted his present to be perfect. It was exactly seven days since she'd driven with Vincent to the airport. Now his apartment was finally ready and waiting for his return. He was due in Saturday, and she was finding it hard to wait. Her mood spilled over to Mark as they waited for the elevator in Vincent's building. They were speculating on what his reaction would be when he opened the door and saw what awaited him.

"I promise to tell you after," she said to Mark as the doors opened. If she'd been alone, Darien would have waited, but with Mark beside her she didn't see the need to let the elevator go just because Mike Guran was on it. But she didn't acknowledge his presence.

"Vincent has no idea and we just have to keep it that way for a few more days."

"I'm not going to say a word," Mark answered, his face serious, yet beaming. He was having as much fun as she was.

It wasn't until they neared the lobby that Mike moved forward, his hip brushing her buttocks. Darien froze, than deliberately swung her large purse to her other shoulder, aiming it and her elbow for Mike's stomach. She felt the impact but didn't turn back, holding back a smile as the air rushed from his lungs. She mumbled an excuse as the doors opened and didn't wait to watch his reaction.
****

"How was your day?" Vincent asked, his back to the conference room that was slowly emptying. He stared at the foreign city below him, longing to be back in New York City beside her.

"Over, thank God, but better now. How's yours going?"

"I called a ten minute break to phone you." Her laugh went straight to his heart.

"I'm sure all your business associates were thrilled when you tossed them out to call your girlfriend, but I'm glad you did. I miss you Vincent. More than I should."

"Keep thinking that way, Darien. I'm going to wrap this up as soon as possible, even if I have to walk away. I'm sick of the game. It's not a challenge any more, just a huge waste of time."

"Maybe we need to find you something new to revive your interests. Any ideas come to mind?" And so their conversation continued, with lust smoldering over the airwaves.

"Too many. That's why I'm annoyed with being here. Tell me how your meeting went with your new clients. Are you going to take them on?" Her deep laugh made him smile. "Tell me."

"It's silly, really. They're a very nice older couple with a new apartment on the west side. The thing is, he's going to let her make all the decisions, and she wants... Oh, Vincent, she wants all basic...tan! The first thing that came to my mind was a cave with a view!" The irony wasn't lost on him and he laughed with her. "Then I decided you and she should swap apartments. Yours would be perfect for her." She continued to laugh.

"I only see one problem with that."

"Wait, let me guess. You changed your mind, and like the monotone scheme?"

"No, but I like the location and the view."

"All, well, there go my best-laid plans. All right, what if we take all your furniture and swap it into her space, and you get a whole new look?"

"That's closer to doable! Are you going to sign them?"

"Yes, they're really a very nice couple and I know what they're looking for, so it won't be a hurried job. And I told them I won't start until after the first of the year. They're having some interior construction done so it will all work out. By the time the contractor is finished, I'll have had time to work out their design details."

"I miss you, Darien."

"I miss you too. Will you be able to get away for Christmas?"

"No doubt, no matter what the outcome here is."

"What would you usually do for Christmas?"

"Generally I go away. Sometimes to ski, other times to a warm beach."

"If you hadn't met me this year what would you have done?" This time his laugh came across the lines.

"I hadn't decided yet."

"I see. So I was a way of avoiding a decision?"

"No, Darien, you were a lifeline I've waited all my life for."

"Thank you, Vincent. Come home," she finished.

"Soon, as soon as I can."

"I'll be waiting."

Chapter Nine

When her intercom rang shortly after eight the next night, Darien became alarmed. She wasn't expecting anyone, and even though she hadn't heard from Vincent tonight, she assumed he was still away. She hit the button but wasn't prepared for the angry voice bellowing at her.

"Darien, let me in!"

She relaxed when she recognized his voice, and hit the outer door lock. She ran to her bathroom, pulled a brush through her hair, and glanced at her overall appearance. It was too late to make any other changes. By the time she made her way back to the hallway, he was literally pounding on her door.

"Darien, let me in!"

Smiling at his overanxiousness, she swung open the door as her arms swept wide to accept him. Then she saw the look on his face. He stormed past her and marched straight to the living room window, his back to her. Something was definitely wrong, but she had no idea what. She drew a deep breath, and moved behind him, reaching to his shoulders. Her hands barely made contact with his wool coat when he jerked away from her. If she'd been standing closer, she would have been knocked down by his need to get away from her touch.

"Vincent, what's wrong? What the hell is going on?" Darien watched his precision movements as he slowly turned. His eyes shone black with a coldness she'd never seen before. It was a cruel look and she instinctively moved back from him.

"That's what I want you to tell me, Darien. What the hell is going on?" His eyes narrowed.

Her hands crossed in front of her, hugging her arms to her suddenly cold body. "You're two days early. What are you doing home so soon?" What was really going through her mind was that she was glad his apartment was done. She would have died if he'd come home early and it wasn't ready. God, she thought, the mess he might have walked into.

"Yes, did I screw up your plans?" His open appraisal was lewd instead of sexual.

"Vincent, obviously something has happened, and until you tell me what I can't begin to help..."

"Obviously. The act doesn't suit you, Darien. God, how could you do this to me? I don't understand, I'll never understand it." His mask of hate slipped and Darien read confusion and hurt before he controlled his emotions.

"Understand what? What have I supposedly done that was so wrong?" His apartment came to mind and she wondered if he'd been home and had hated what she had done? Only a flicker of sad recognition passed over her face but it was enough for him to latch onto with his anger. Cautiously she inched a step closer. And for the second time he shunned her touch, a look of total disgust apparent on his features.

"Just what have I supposedly done that was so wrong, Vincent? Maybe you should clue me in." She held her ground and stared at him. His chest rose and fell with several long breaths before he finally answered.

"Must I spell it out for you, Darien? You were caught in the act."

"Doing what?" Her voice rose and she tried to tame it back.

"And with Mark, my assistant, of all people. Was it because he's younger than me? God, how stupid a man am I?"

"Mark? What's he got to do with this? Just what was I supposedly caught doing? Stop talking in circles so we can figure this out, please?"

"Why my place, Darien? Why not bring him here, or to a hotel? Why did you have to flaunt it in my home?" He straightened and took a step back.

She had no idea what was really going on, but there had to be a terrible mistake and if she could get to the bottom of it, she could fix it. Giving them both a bit of space, she went to the kitchen where she pulled glasses from the cabinet, then filled them with ice and sparkling water. He was back at the window when she returned. She placed a glass on the window sill in front of him and withdrew.

"Vincent, tell me exactly what I have done to hurt you. Please?" She tried to keep her voice level, the fear mixed with repressed anger.

"Did it thrill you to take your lover into my home and screw him in my bed, Darien? Did it give you both an extra high to know how you both were belittling me?"

"Vincent, I don't know what you think happened, but it's not what it looks like. Your information is wrong." Now she had to make a decision. Did she tell him about her redecorating efforts or send him away because he was a jerk? The longer she thought about it, the more she decided he was an ass, and that fed her anger and heated her temper. Vincent didn't trust her. It all came down to those four simple words.

"You were seen, Darien, both of you. Talk your way out of that one."

"No, I won't. Yes, I was at your apartment while you were away, and Mark met me there twice." She refused to tell him why. He didn't trust her. If he did, he would have questioned the rumor instead of putting her through his version of the Inquisition with attitude. She'd never seen him so angry. His nasty side had been well hidden during their time together. This side was a man she didn't want to be near.

"So you admit to the affair?"

"No, I admit to being in your building and your apartment. I never slept with Mark."

"Darien, do you really think I'm that much of an ass?"

"I'm beginning to, Vincent. Have you been home yet, or did you come straight here from landing?"

"No, I came straight here to take care of business. I don't care if I ever see the place again. You tainted it, Darien. I'll never be comfortable there again." He took the glass she'd placed before him and drank greedily. That was when she noticed he was rubbing his temples. She slipped away to get him some aspirin. He'd compose himself. They'd talk it all through, and one day they'd laugh about the whole mess. She grabbed the bottle instead of a few pills and returned to place it near his water glass.

Vincent shook out three into his palm and swallowed them with the last of his water. He didn't acknowledge her peace offering. Instead, he glanced around her apartment.

"Vincent, do you really think I took Mark as a lover while you were out of town for a week and used your apartment for our supposed tryst?"

"Yes, Darien, I do."

"Why? Why would I do such a stupid thing? It doesn't make sense if you think it through."

"It does to me. Right from the start you played me, Darien. Not accepting my drink offer at the auction but stalling outside long enough to meet me. Was it because you lost the bar or did it go deeper? Was the bar ever the issue, or was it the property in Glen Cove? How long did you work to set it all up?"

"You think I set up the meeting at the auction?

You think I deliberately insinuated myself into your life?"

"Yes, I do."

She stared at him, her mind reeling. She needed to organize her thoughts. "Where did you get this information? Who told you I was there and what exactly did they say?" He only stared at her and she tried a different approach. "Just to get this straight—you think the bar was incidental to losing the property to you. That I slept with you for the property?"

"Yes, I do."

Something deep inside her snapped with his words. "Get out, go home, Vincent," she told him in a low trembling voice.

"Oh no, not until I've had my say. I'm the injured party, Darien."

"And I invited you home for the holidays to meet my parents to continue the charade?" She couldn't believe this was happening.

"It all makes sense. I was a means to an end."

"And what end would that be?"

"I believe you figured you'd eventually get the property and ultimately the house you wanted built." He held her eye and she didn't look away. For tense seconds they stared at each other, neither of them daring to blink.

"That's enough! Go home, Vincent. *Get out...*" This time she didn't try to rein in her resentment, and it was Vincent who took a step back.

"I am going, Darien, and I'm leaving a wiser man."

"You're leaving as an asshole, Vincent. Just leave," she said, exasperated.

He stared her down, but she refused to be intimidated. He all but pushed past her, heading out. She followed him when she realized Mark was in jeopardy. He'd made it to the elevator when she called to him, "Vincent, what are you going to do about Mark?" She watched him freeze and finally turn back.

"I'm sure you'll save me the trouble. You'll be on the telephone as soon as I'm gone. I doubt he'll have the balls to show up at the office tomorrow."

"Vincent, don't do anything stupid that you can't take back, please. Tonight is bad enough. Don't make it worse. Go home and think it all through."

"Don't dictate to me, Darien. I can't believe you went after him. He's just a kid. He never stood a chance with a woman like you. Maybe the term harlot was more accurate than I ever imagined. Did you tip off the tabloid, Darien?"

"Stop it, Vincent. Just go home."

"I almost bought it, Darien. Almost asked you to marry me and spend the rest of our lives together. Almost. You should have held out a little longer. The divorce settlement would have seen you through years. Knowing this, I'd rather see the lot go vacant for the rest of my life than put a house there now. And no matter what, I'll make sure you never see it again."

"Vincent, you've said enough. Just go and don't come back. You don't know what you're talking about. If you really think I'm capable of this whole plan you've decided I put together, then you don't know me at all."

"I never really did know you, Darien, did I? I only knew the side you exposed to trap me. I will thank you for the reality check. Next time I start to have feelings for a woman I'll make sure to stop cold in my tracks and walk away. This whole situation is crazy and out of line, but it was educational. I can't believe I trusted you with so much..."

"And I didn't trust you?" She fought for control. "Where did this information come from? Who told you I was having an affair with Mark at your apartment?"

"None of it matters anymore." And she knew he was right. Their bond had been broken and she didn't see any way to mend it. Best she let him walk away now before he hurt her any further. Once he realized she wasn't having an affair with Mark, he'd have to deal with his temper and the repercussions.

"No, it doesn't. Good-bye, Vincent." She turned and left him at the elevator, closing her apartment door behind her. Only then did she allow the tears to well up and overflow down her cheeks. Only then did she allow the gravity of the situation to drift forward and hit her with a reality check.

Vincent didn't trust her, and now he was gone. She'd hurt for a while, probably a long time, but it was for the best. Right from the beginning she'd had reservations and tried to tell him, but he was so sure, so overpowering with his affection toward her. She'd accept some of the blame for their failed relationship, but not all.

Oh, how she wished she could be there later when he walked into his apartment and saw what she was really doing there with Mark. Dropping onto her bed, she let herself have a good cry. She glanced at the telephone several times and knew he wouldn't call. His ego wouldn't allow him to, no matter what. Several regrets came to mind. Sharing her body with him was the first, and the second was one of the presents she'd left under the tree.

Chapter Ten

Vincent disliked the doorman's overanxious greeting when he arrived home. The only thing he could think was that the entire building knew of Darien's affair, and he was now a laughingstock. That was simple enough to change. He'd move. He doubted he'd ever be able to walk into the space again and not visualize them together. All he had to do was pack his clothes and he'd be free. He'd leave the apartment just as he found it, selling it turnkey. Good luck to the next person who wanted to live in a tan enclave.

The idea struck him to locate Darien's latest customer and sell it to her, thereby alleviating his need to sell the apartment *and* deny a commission for Darien. His stomach twisted at the revenge aspect of his thoughts and he almost mellowed. The whole situation made him start to second guess the information before remembering the mention of their closeness during their conversation at his cocktail party. Somehow he couldn't visualize Darien in Mark's arms, but it didn't matter.

He had to decide between two hotels and knew in the morning he'd make arrangements for a long-term stay. The elevator jerked to a stop at his floor. He could look for a new place after the holidays. The long walk down the hallway was filled with the image of Darien and Mark standing together in the corner on the night of his party. He was certain she started laying her groundwork then, remembering how animated Mark had become at her attention. He slipped the key in the door and dragged his suitcase into the foyer. Behind him, the door slammed.

He automatically hit the light switch. Only then did he stop to look ahead of him. Only then did he realize what a jackass he really was. Tossing his keys on the side table, he stared ahead into the winter wonderland his apartment had been turned into. Shrugging off his overcoat, he let it drop to the marble entry floor and dared to take a step further into the room. Everything twinkled with white and colored lights.

Vincent stood in the entry to his living room, totally astonished. Before the windows was a huge decorated Christmas tree. The mantel was covered with fresh pine and multicolored lights. Ribbons and bows were laced through it. The coffee table held a small winter village to scale, complete with a mirrored skating rink and fake snow dusting tree branches. There were potted poinsettias in every empty corner.

Even the draperies over the window hadn't been left out. There were swags of garland and roping interspersed with more lights. What impressed him most was the overall picture. Behind a club chair, hidden with more plants, was a spotlight with a revolving four-color plate. With each revolution, the white lights on the tree took on a different color. Overwhelming, to say the least. His weary mind moved on overload.

Vincent turned in the space several more times, noticing small touches here and there. It was magnificent. The room could have held its own with any department store window. And she'd done it for him, because he told her his best memories of the holiday weren't the presents, it was the traditions. He let his hand run over one of the tree limbs, pulling off a few of the needles. Crushing them between his fingers, he inhaled the pine scent they released. Instantly, Vincent knew the doorman was greeting him differently because they must have known what she was doing. No way could she have gotten the tree past all of them, and what one doorman knew, they all did.

How long had she worked? How many people did it take to accomplish this in less than a week? Automatically he moved to the telephone, and then put it down. She'd never answer her phone tonight, no matter what he said to her machine. Now he knew why she was so curious if he'd come home first or gone straight to see her.

Vincent sat on the corner of his sofa for a long time, watching each light twinkle, memorizing each ornament and figurine she'd placed around. His favorites were the Mr. and Mrs. Claus gracing the mantel. While they were only about two feet tall, their porcelain faces had been beautifully painted, their costumes painstakingly recreated. Their hands were locked together. Vincent forced himself from the seat, moving to his bedroom. He flipped on the light switch and dropped his bag in the hallway, taking a tentative step into the room.

She had made changes in his bedroom too. Gone were the tan bedspread and matching upholstered chair and loveseat. The bed was now covered with a silk comforter in a green and gold swirl pattern. The loveseat was covered with a coordinated striped silk. The club chair boasted a soft green tapestry. Small pillows added extra color and texture. Soft-looking afghans were draped in a few places, and throw rugs on top of the wall-to-wall carpeting pulled it all together. It reminded him of the scarf she wore the first night he brought her there. When he turned, he realized she used it as a pattern for the room. She'd been right on target.

While she hadn't changed any furniture, she'd covered chairs and changed his bedding. The draperies were still tan, but now had a two-tiered overlay disguising them. He wandered into his master bath out of sheer curiosity. It too had been left intact, only towels and linens changed to coordinate with the bedroom. The effect was mind-boggling. Vincent moved out of the pristine space and went to the nearest guest room. There he stripped and took a long hot shower, and tried to decide what to do. Nothing came to mind, depressing him further. How stupid he'd been to assume she was cheating on him, especially with Mark.

"God, I'm *such* an ass!" he told his reflection in the mirror. Back in his room, he grabbed a pair of sweatpants from a drawer and pulled them on. Pushing his hair from his eyes, he went back to the living room where he sat on his sofa, his sofa that looked completely different with the addition of emerald, sapphire, and ruby-colored pillows. He lay down and surveyed at the room around him. Even to his untrained eye, he knew once the holiday decorations were packed away the space would still reflect her style.

Vincent Leighton, who hadn't shed a tear since his grandmother had died, let himself weep in the darkness. It wasn't until early morning when he was dressing to go to the office that he realized the wrapped boxes under the tree weren't just for display.

There were several, one large carton and another smaller one beside it. Both were heavy when he picked them up. The tags read they were For Vincent, From Santa. A third one looked more like a shirt box but was too heavy to be clothing. Carefully, he placed them back under the tree and moved away.

****

Mark was obviously startled to see Vincent in his office when he arrived for work the next morning. Armed with two mugs, Mark moved quietly into the private office.

"Welcome back. You're a day early. How did the trip go?"

Vincent hoped Mark hadn't watched his expression turn grim as he put the mug in front of him.

"Vincent?" He got no verbal answer. "Have you been home yet?" he tried.

"Yes, Mark. Tell one of the secretaries to cover the telephone and come back."

"Well, you've been home. What do you think?" He searched Vincent's face for a clue as to what was happening; he got none. Finally, he said, "You hated it," accepting defeat. "I'm sorry. I shouldn't have let her in the apartment. I know I only have your key for emergencies, but it sounded like such a great idea, and Darien was so excited to give you a...Vincent?" Again, Mark got no response. "Mr. Leighton?"

Vincent finally looked up at his young protégée. "Sit. Tell me everything from the start, and don't leave out a single detail. It's important."

Mark squirmed in his seat before relating the facts. Vincent leaned back in his large chair, crossing one ankle over his other knee, and listened. Mark's version was that Darien had come to the office last week, asking for his help. She wanted access to the apartment to bring in decorations and make it an old-fashioned holiday home for him. She'd apparently spent the last seven days pulling it all together. He went on to tell him about her trying to get the ten-foot tree into the service elevator, and carting around a six-foot aluminum ladder. Mark told Vincent he'd offered himself for manual labor, but she'd told him this was part of Vincent's Christmas gift. She wanted to do it for him herself. She did apparently let him see it when she was done. That was when she returned the key.

"I'm very sorry, Mr. Leighton," he said when he finished. "I overstepped your trust with your home."

"Yes, technically you did, but I'm not upset at that. Tell me and think clearly. Who else saw you and Darien together in the building?"

"The doormen and the old lady that smells like dead flowers from a few floors down—the one with the mangy-looking poodle."

"That's all? Are you sure?"

"We shared a cab across town the night I picked up the key. I think that's all." Mark started to rub his temples as if in deep thought. "I think that's all, except for the elevator."

"What happened?"

"That last night, Mike Guran was on the elevator with us. The guy you had me delete from all the guest lists. I've got to say that Darien handled him well."

"What did he do or say?"

"Nothing really. He didn't say anything. It was more the way he looked at her. When we were nearing the lobby, I noticed him getting closer to her, but she used her purse to push him away. Actually she elbowed him in the stomach and used her purse as an excuse. He stepped back after that." Mark was confused and Vincent figured he was sure he was about to get fired. Vincent burst out laughing and Mark fidgeted in his seat.

Vincent watched the strange look that crossed Mark's face and pulled himself together. "Relax. I'm not going to fire you, but you're going to help me fix this."

"Fix what? Don't you like the apartment?"

"I love the apartment, but...I jumped to some wrong conclusions." Vincent only briefly explained about the telephone call he'd received and how he'd burst in on Darien, accusing her of having an affair with Mark in his apartment. He saw the horrified look on the young man's face and wanted to kick himself for letting the situation get out of control.

"I'm sorry, Vincent. She's a lovely lady but I wouldn't stand a chance with her. And I'd never put a move on someone you loved. I admit I'm attracted to her, but she stands a full head taller than me, not to mention that she's head over heels in love with you. Why, everything she did was to make your holiday better. And I'm almost insulted that you would believe I could betray you like that after all you've done for me." His face reddened with anger as he spoke.

"I'm sorry, Mark. I was wrong. Now I have to figure out how to fix this and get Darien back."

"I'd be careful. If you really pissed her off, you're in deep trouble! When a lady like Darien falls in love, she doesn't go away quietly." He shook his head from side to side to punctuate his words.

"I agree, and believe me, I more than pissed her off last night."

"Oh, boss, what are you gonna do?"

The perplexed look on Mark's face almost made Vincent relax. He held back a smile, thinking Mark would do enough worrying for both of them. A second glance and he wanted to kick himself yet another time. Not only about Darien, but for believing Mark would betray him.

"I'm not sure just yet. But this doesn't leave this office. Only you, me, Darien, and the person who made the phone call know about it. That's the way it stays."

"I got it. Not a word." Vincent gave him a dismissive nod and turned to look out the window, lost in thought before Mark even left the room.

****

"Vincent, I'm sorry to interrupt. I thought you should know…"

"What is it, Mark?"

143

"Darien just called. She wanted to make sure I didn't lose my job for helping her. I told her there wasn't a problem."

He added a lethargic, "And?"

"And I asked her if she wanted to talk to you and she said no."

"Thanks."

"Vincent, it's none of my business, but it sounded like she'd been crying." He watched as his boss sat back in his seat and took in the information he'd relayed. When he got no further response, he left quietly, closing the door after him. Only minutes later, Vincent stormed past Mark's desk while pulling on his coat.

"I'm gone for the day, but I have my cell phone. Only if it's important, got it?"

"Got it. I'll see you on Monday unless you need me before."

"No, have a good weekend. I'll see you next week."

Outside the cold penetrated his wool overcoat. He found himself walking down Madison Avenue, only he was too distracted to notice the decorations this time. He finally glanced at the store windows he'd passed with Darien just a week before, remembering how easily she laughed with him, how she fit against his body, how she loved him so completely and selflessly. He drew back a wave of tears, pulling his sunglasses from his pocket to hide his eyes. His times with Darien had been the best he'd had in years. She made him feel wanted, and most of all she made him feel loved.

He walked across the street and into the old church on the opposite corner. He didn't care what denomination it was. He just wanted the atmosphere and a quiet place to think and get his life together.

****

When the intercom rang, she knew it would be

Vincent. There was no escaping him, so she decided it would be better to face him now and get it over with.

"Darien, can I come up?"

She hit the button, then propped open her hallway door. She walked to the farthest point in the space, the living room window, and stared at the street below. It was obvious she'd been crying and she didn't try to hide it from him. He dropped the three dozen red tulips on the dining room table and crossed to her, stopping a few feet behind her.

"Darien, I'm sorry. I was wrong not to trust you."

"Yes, you were. It was a big mistake, Vincent."

"I have no excuse. I came in here half-cocked on bad information. I lost my cool when I heard you and Mark had been in my apartment."

"It doesn't matter anymore. It's over."

"You're wrong, Darien. It matters more than you could ever imagine." They were both quiet for a time. He didn't bother to take off his coat. She was glad he understood he wouldn't be staying long.

The worst part was letting him see what his mistrust had done. As she turned, she knew he'd see her puffy eyes and tearstained cheeks. She needed him to know he'd hurt her in a place that was beyond repair with a few flowers.

"I'd like to get a few things straight, and then I'd like you to leave, all right?" If there was one thing Darien knew, it was that she wanted to clear her name and her reputation, even if it was just for herself. She needed to be able to face him in the future and not be ashamed or intimidated, not if she was going to stay in New York. And she wasn't going to let this episode run her from the town she loved. She'd square things with Vincent and then walk away with her head up and shoulders back.

"Yes, anything to make this better."

"Is Mark's job or his future in jeopardy for helping me?"

"No, not at all."

"Do you understand now why I was in your building?"

"Yes, of course. You were turning my drab apartment into a winter wonderland of a home. And Darien, it's magnificent. Better than any window display we saw. I never imagined your mind worked that way."

She caught a hint of excitement in his voice and wished she'd been able to give him his gift as planned.

"Is there any chance you'd forgive me and forget I was an ass last night?

Darien gave him half a smile but pulled herself up short from warming to him. "You're a little too late for that, Vincent. Last night, if you had talked to me, we could have straightened it all out." She turned her back on him before adding, "You should have trusted me, no questions asked, until you had all the facts."

"Yes, you're right."

She glanced over her shoulder and nodded to the tulips. "Are they for me?"

"Yes, a pathetic attempt to get your attention so you'd talk to me."

"Thanks. I suppose there's no reason to let them die." Darien moved past him and into the kitchen. When she didn't return shortly, he went to the doorway. Darien hated that he saw her leaning on the counter as a fresh wave of tears spilled down her cheeks.

He slowly wrapped his arms around her. "Darien, I'm so sorry. I was so wrong."

"Yes, you were." She reluctantly moved from his embrace and grabbed the vase from the sink before walking away. Neither of them mentioned the large splash of water that swirled over the rim to puddle on the kitchen floor. At the dining room table she arranged the stems in the crystal vase, her hands shaking with each movement. Darien realized it was the first time he'd really seen her mad, and at him. Angry and hurt seemed to fit her emotional state. He'd done this.

"Is there any way you could give me a second chance?"

"Vincent, it would never work. You'll never trust me enough to give me the automatic belief I need from my partner. I may be naïve, but I want what my parents have, that unconditional love and trust no matter what happens. I need to be your first priority in any and all circumstances, just as I would put you first."

"I could work on it."

She almost smiled at him. "It's my fault, too. I never should have let us get this far. I knew from the start you'd hurt me. But it was like I didn't have a choice with you. My good judgment and common sense just floated away when I looked at you. When you're near me, I have no resistance."

"I didn't mean to blow up. I got the phone call and all I could see was red. There was no black or white or even gray."

"That's just my point. You didn't believe I loved you or you never would have accepted a stranger's words without at least asking me what the situation was."

"Darien, give me a second chance. Please?"

"No. It's time for you to leave." She held his eye and watched him take a step back in retreat.

"All the changes in the apartment. I want you to live there with me and enjoy them."

"Maybe once it might have been possible, but not now." She glanced toward the hall door and back to him. He took her hint and headed toward it. She stayed a few feet away from him, her hands twisting in front of her. "As adults, we make choices and I'm choosing not to let you hurt me again."

"I'll fight for you, Darien. I'll make a bigger ass of myself if I have to. Newspaper ads, billboards, anything to get you back."

She gave him a horrified look. "And give the tabloids more fuel? No, please don't do that. Trust me. It would make this much worse."

"If you think of a way for me to make amends, call me. I'll do almost anything to get you back."

This time she did smile, even though it was a sad smile. She moved beside him, her hands angling his face toward her.

"Vincent, you'll never really know how much I love you. You'll never accept it unconditionally from me, and I need it back from you. It's not there, or we wouldn't be in this mess right now." Darien leaned up on her toes and let her lips touch his in a brief kiss. "Good-bye, Vincent."

"Darien, please?"

"You have to leave now. It's best for us both. I hope you find what you're looking for. You deserve to be happy." She leaned past him and opened the hall door further. He took her dismissal reasonably well, considering the circumstances. Once he was in the hall, she hesitated before shutting her door. He grabbed her, pulling her to him, pressing her against the length of him. She didn't pull away for a long time, but when she did, she felt cold and hollow. "Vincent, please go. I've earned at least that. Don't make me beg you to leave."

"Just ask me to stay instead." He let the corners of his mouth curl into a slight smile, adding, "It was worth a try."

"Goodbye, Vincent." She pulled back and finally closed the door—closing herself in her own private hell, away from him.

Chapter Eleven

Vincent hated Christmas. The day dragged by, each hour seeming like four. He'd refused several invitations knowing he wouldn't be good company. Worse would be to force the smiles and cheerful tone expected of him. All of Darien's holiday lights were turned on, even the rotating spotlight. He hadn't bothered to turn on the television or the radio. Instead, he'd opened a bottle of expensive scotch, pouring some into his morning coffee. By noon he'd given up on adding the coffee, drinking it straight. By four o'clock, he'd drunk himself straight.

He dozed on the sofa for a while, waking with a terrible hangover, his head pounding out a self-imposed steady beat. When a shower didn't help, he forced himself into the kitchen, making a sandwich. Vincent ate it standing over the kitchen sink as his empty stomach adjusted to its new state. Along with it he downed two bottles of water and several aspirin. Knowing the agony was by his own hand, Vincent decided punishing himself physically wasn't for him. His mind was vivid enough without wasting his physical condition. He stayed there a long time, his head in his hand leaning on the counter, wondering what Darien was doing at that very moment.

She was all around him. Even her scent still lingered in the air after all this time, though he never felt her scent was overpowering when she was with him. These lingering hints were memories to torture him further. Or, he surmised, his mind conjured up her scent to comfort him. Surprisingly, he was beginning to accept his screw-up and that he might not get her back. It wasn't a concept he was ready to concede but he was beginning to accept that it might be an option she took.

Remote control in hand, he laid back on the sofa in his study, flipping channels to keep his mind busy. Nothing suited him or his mood. He'd picked up his telephone several times during the day, each time putting it aside, knowing his call would be mainly for himself, not her. Darien would still be hurt. Her parents would know and hate him too. Without meeting them, he knew enough about Darien and her family in the abstract to know their holiday wasn't full of smiles and laughs. He knew his present had arrived at her parents' house in Chicago because Mark had verified the delivery. So, she had his present, and she still hadn't called him. Even if she never did speak to him again, he still wanted her to have it. After all, he'd had it made for her.

When the eleven o'clock news went off the air, he finally conceded she wasn't going to call. Only then did he pull the three packages with his name on them from under the tree. Vincent opened the largest one first, the hint of child in him shining through. It turned out to be a beautifully carved mahogany humidor, only instead of being filled with cigars; it was stuffed with packs of his favorite imported cigarettes. He couldn't stop smiling while remembering them sharing one on his balcony the first night they were together.

The second present made him laugh out loud. He didn't know how she knew, except that she must have read his mind somewhere along the way. He'd never mentioned it to her. He hadn't told anyone else, even Mark. He pulled the statue from the protective packaging. It stood about eighteen inches tall overall. A Christmas tree decorated with glass ornaments and flocked with snow covered branches was anchored to a wood platform, with several brightly wrapped packages tucked under it to complete the display. Beside it was a hand-painted porcelain three-dimensional sculpture of Betty Page, kneeling beside the tree, a present in her hands. She wore a Santa cap, a smile, and nothing else.

It was beautifully done, not vulgar as it might have been. Instead, the detailing was incredible and her proportions correct. Vincent didn't know where Darien found her but he loved it. It told him so much about her, how she understood him and was able to convey it with a sense of humor. He held the statue for a long time before carefully placing her on the mantel.

Vincent sat in the darkened room, lit only by the mini-lights and watched the night sky. The third box was still on his lap, waiting to be opened. He didn't know if he had the emotional strength to continue. Ultimately, his curiosity won out and he found himself tearing at the paper. What he pulled from the shirt box was no piece of clothing. "Oh, my God," he whispered, carefully handling the antique silver picture frame, classic with a beaded edge. Framed in it was a photograph of Millner Farm, dated 1973.

It blew him away to see the house in its original form. He stared at it for a long time before placing it aside and finally letting himself cry over her a second time. When his emotions settled, he studied the photo, realizing Darien's design had incorporated the best parts of the original farmhouse as well as some of his original concept. Stan's theory was still present but Darien's touches and ideas brought it all together.

She truly loved this land and the long-gone home. Apparently he'd taken it away from her twice now. The first time he was unsuspecting, the second time he'd ripped the house and her heart from her by not trusting in her love. He'd accepted the gossip of a third party and lost everything. What frustrated and infuriated him most of all was that Mike Guran had made the call. It ate at his insides, a situation he'd have to handle eventually, but he wanted to put some thought into how to best go about it.

****

The Monday after Christmas he'd been happy to head back to the office. He forced himself to leave the apartment after his self-indulgent binge on Christmas day, spending hours at the gym, punishing himself for all the things he'd screwed up. Vincent refused to look at any of the other people spending their day the same way. He didn't want to look into their eyes and see the loneliness he felt.

Since Vincent had planned to be away this week, the office was technically on vacation until after the first. The small bonus was one all his employees enjoyed. In past years he'd taken himself away, usually somewhere warm where he spent the holiday season. The phones barely rang while he walked the empty hallways. A service was set up to handle any incoming calls so he let them ring. He sat in the huge chair behind his massive desk wondering where his life was going.

When his cell phone rang he answered it, disappointed that the security desk was letting him know a messenger was on his way up with a package. He'd signed for it and knew instantly what was inside. The Chicago return address was that of the West home. He tossed it into his briefcase, forcing himself back to the gym. Not until late that night did he allow himself to open it.

As he expected, Darien had returned his gift. Opening the velvet box, he looked at the necklace he'd had designed for her. The square center emerald was four carats surrounded by diamonds, all suspended from a heavy gold chain, fixed in the center so it wouldn't shift on her neck. Attached was a note in her bold black print. He might as well read it and move on.

Dear Vincent,

While the necklace is magnificent, we both know I can't keep it.

I truly wish things had turned out differently for us, and I'm sorry for any hurt I caused you. I wish you only wonderful things for your future.

Darien

He pulled the stones from their nest, holding them in his hand for a long time, before ultimately dropping the necklace back in the box and sealing it away in the wall safe. The only act of courage he could commend himself for was that he didn't take out the other small box, torturing himself by staring at the engagement ring he'd had made at the same time. He knew what it looked like; it was the companion to the necklace, only with the stones reversed. The diamond centered the ring and was flanked with emeralds. He went to bed that night not knowing where his future lay, only that he'd never be the same.

****

Darien dressed carefully for the New Year's Eve celebration she wouldn't skip. While she was home for Christmas, she'd told her parents the whole sordid tale of her relationship with Vincent and the ultimate demise by an unknown outside force. They managed to cheer her up and refrained from giving her any advice on her love life. Her mother had taken her aside the last day she was there, asking her what she planned to do to ring in the New Year. Darien told her about the yearly bash the Dawkins held at a hotel near Central Park. They debated her going or staying home. By the time she was landing in New York, she knew she'd attend, just to prove to herself Vincent hadn't broken her spirit.

Her silver halter dress was trimmed with small green beads, the bodice shot with them in a random pattern. It was the dress of her dreams. She knew she looked great. It emphasized her ample bustline but wasn't low-cut. It was tapered at her slim waist, flowing over her hips to just above her knees. Pairing it with silver evening shoes and purse, Darien tossed the velvet cape over her shoulders. Her hair was piled high on her head and she wore only diamond stud earrings and bracelets.

She'd applied her makeup with a heavy hand, trying to conceal the dark circles under her eyes. Knowing Vincent would be there was her motivation to push for a polished look. It wouldn't do to let him see what he'd done to her. Dread coursed through her each time she wondered if he'd bring a date. Deciding he wouldn't, she realized she'd thought just recently that she knew and loved this man, and look what happened!

****

There was no mistaking his entrance. In a subdued black tuxedo, he entered the party as women's heads turned. She watched him from across the crowded room as he greeted his hosts and accepted a drink from a passing waiter. She also watched him zero in on her, heading in her direction. For the first hour she was there she thought he might have changed his mind and not come; now she knew he'd waited to make sure she was there. Several people stopped him along the way, and she knew he was being polite but short with them. Stationed by the balcony, she slipped through the doors when he was sidetracked by another woman. The woman seemed intent on telling him something so funny, she had to place her hand on his arm to steady her. Darien felt her stomach somersault and decided she'd witnessed enough of the spectacle. All she had to do was get through the next half hour and then she could slip away. It wasn't to be.

****

"The air up here always smells so much cleaner," he said from behind her. "You look beautiful, Darien."

She didn't turn to greet him. Instead she became very interested in the street below. "Thank you," she managed, her voice sounding steady, so she continued, wishing she hadn't as soon as she spoke. "You okay?" Darien bit her lip as the words escaped. The last thing she wanted was him to know she was still thinking of him. More importantly, she didn't want him to know he mattered or how much. He moved beside her at the railing, a few feet of politically correct space between them.

"Are we telling the truth or lying?" He smiled when she laughed at his question.

"Your choice," she answered, and was sorry she turned to look at him. Even in the darkness he was handsome. His nose was still crooked, and his chin almost too long, but his full mouth and lips evened out his profile. The intense look in his eyes made her want to throw her arms around his neck and pull him to her. How could she not love him?

"I've been lying low. The office was closed this week."

"I'm still not adjusted from being in another time zone." Vincent thought to ask how her holiday went, but knew it wasn't a topic he should introduce. Mainly because he didn't want to hear her answer. Even if she lied and told him it was fine, he knew it hadn't been, and that he was the cause. While she looked perfect to outside eyes, he saw the sorrow in her look, and knew he'd put it there. A shudder passed through her under his scrutiny.

"Darien, aren't you cold?" he asked. When she didn't answer him, he changed the subject. "What did you tell Sissy about us?"

"Nothing, really. I made it seem that we were just acquaintances, and she'd been the one to blow our relationship out of proportion as well as the tabloid." He laughed openly and she let him enjoy the irony. "It seemed a better defense than explaining. I let her think our romance was in her mind."

"How did she take it?" For an instant, his old Darien was beside him. She had to pull back.

"'Confused' comes to mind as a descriptive word." The shared a laugh as co-conspirators.

"Good. Keep her that way. Thank you for handling her, Darien."

"No problem, I really do like her, now that I'm not her employee. She's a kind woman, but a little overanxious at times." Darien felt the cold start to chill her and moved away from the railing. Enough was enough. She'd let everyone see she was fine. Now she could escape. "Vincent, I have to go." He didn't answer but changed the subject.

"One dance, Darien. It's almost midnight, and you'll never get a cab. One dance, and I'll have my driver bring you home, if that's what you still want."

"That's probably not a good idea, Vincent. I should just leave now."

He watched her face and for an instant thought she might start to cry. Instead, she lowered her head for only a second before standing tall and turning to leave. He didn't resist the impulse to reach to her, turning her directly into his arms. The warmth of his body against the cold of hers had them both holding tight without realizing they were locked in each other's arms. The music in the background filtered toward them.

"I don't care if it's a good idea. Do it anyway, Darien. Please?" He released her from his hold but not from his arms. She would have been able to walk away if he hadn't added the 'please.' It didn't matter.

She was in his arms swaying against his body to the music and she never wanted the song to end. When it changed, his fingers tightened around her, keeping her close for one more dance. Vincent thought to thank her for his Christmas gifts and decided to wait for another time, fearing reality would have her pulling from his embrace.

Midnight on New Year's Eve in Manhattan was always loud. When the noise started around them, neither moved. Vincent let his head drop to press his lips to hers. Reminiscent of their first kiss outside the blues club after the auction, he didn't plunder her mouth. It was Darien who deepened the kiss, her tongue sliding against his lips, parting them for entry. Darien kissed Vincent with all the emotion she'd stored up since their confrontation. She pulled back from him when she realized it was a kiss of things to come, not a kiss good-bye or just for midnight on New Year's.

He hesitated to let her go. When her body left contact with his, he was suddenly cold. She'd already gotten lost in the crowded room by the time he followed her inside, waiting while his erection subsided. Chasing after her wasn't the best idea, not now, anyway. Her kiss had surprised him. He assumed she'd struggle away from his touch when in reality she'd given him the emotional ride he missed so much.

The small smirk stayed on his lips as he moved to the hallway, telephoning downstairs to his driver. He knew she'd get her ride home and he wouldn't worry. He also knew not to follow her right now. Instead, he smiled and was polite for another forty minutes until his driver phoned him he was back and Darien safely home.

****

Darien was relieved when she made it down to the lobby without being stopped. She'd avoided Sissy

157

and Lyle and headed toward the ladies' room. Only after getting herself together did she move to the cloak room and gather her cape. Downstairs she would ask the doorman to get her a cab, even if it took awhile. She cursed the evening shoes she knew she didn't want to walk home in, all right, dreaded walking anywhere in, but they did match the dress. She was thrilled to recognize Vincent's car and driver waiting at the entrance.

The driver only nodded as he opened the rear door. She slipped into the warmed compartment, letting her head drop back against the seat. It was over. She'd managed to get through the evening, and survived not only their first confrontation, but dancing and kissing him one last time. Both things she did for herself, not him.

Chapter Twelve

The museum project had once meant a lot to him. He'd spent countless hours organizing and raising funds for the new collection. He was proud to see it gracing the walls of the old structure, knowing he had a hand in its inception. The only thing that might have made his success better was Darien standing by his side, wearing not only his necklace but his engagement ring too. It wasn't to be.

She'd been invited but had RSVPed that she wouldn't be attending. Not that she spoke to him. She sent a short note to Mark's attention with her regrets. Taking another look around the lobby filled with the people who had helped make the night a reality with their donations, he knew she wouldn't slip in. The dedication and speeches behind him, he took his first glass of wine from a passing waiter's tray, enjoying the cold, crisp flavor. He only had to last another hour or so. Then this would all be over and he could go home.

Only home wasn't the same anymore. If he'd thought it staid and boring before Darien, now it was lifeless and depressing. He hadn't taken down any of the decorations, leaving a perpetual state of Christmas to return to each night. It was a form of self-imposed misery he couldn't seem to stop. Vincent had never really considered himself a glutton for punishment before, but he understood this was right somehow at this time. The irony was the comfort it gave him.

The tree was on its last legs. He knew it had to go but couldn't bring himself to take it down. Even his housekeeper had mentioned in the last week that it was well past Christmas and turning into a fire hazard. He'd snapped at her to keep it watered and let it alone. She did just that, not mentioning it again. All he wanted after a long, distracted day at the office was a longer evening to go home and stare at the damn thing. Mark interrupted his thoughts and he checked his watch again.

Just when he'd had enough of smiling and thanking people, he spotted Sissy heading toward him. Earlier he'd glided past her and Lyle several times, avoiding any real personal conversation. Now he knew it was inevitable. Best to get it over with, he decided, then he'd slip away.

"Sissy, you're beautiful as always. Lyle, thanks again for your support."

Their small talk was strained until Sissy pointed out an old friend to Lyle, telling him to go ahead and she'd join him in a minute. Vincent watched as the other man walked away with a knowing look, accepting his dismissal, and taking advantage of it. He also knew there was no use trying to get away from her until she'd said what was on her mind. He gave her a polite smile as they watched Lyle disappear into the crowd.

"How are you, really?" she asked bluntly.

"Fine, Sissy, just glad this is behind us. It was a lot of work, but..." She cut him off with the wave of her diamond-appointed hand.

"I'm not talking about the museum, and we both know it, Vincent." She held his eye and suddenly he had a new respect for her, even if he was on the wrong side of her suspicions. He remembered what Darien said on New Year's Eve and decided to stick with the story.

"What then?" He brought the wine to his lips but only to moisten them. Suddenly it didn't appeal anymore, but he held it anyway as a prop.

"You look like you've been through the mill, Vincent. It's not attractive."

"Thank you, Sissy," he replied with a laugh.

"It's a shame Darien couldn't attend tonight."

"Yes, she had a previous engagement," he started, watching her study him, knowing she didn't believe him.

"I don't know what previous engagement she might have had, but I know it changed the day before yesterday." Sissy held his eye with a steely stare. Vincent finally accepted she was trying to tell him something.

"Sissy, I'd prefer to leave Darien's private life out of our conversation." He glared back at her and she laughed in his face. She laughed again when he stiffened beside her.

"Vincent, I really am growing to like you. You try so hard; but you're not asking the correct question." Her exaggerated, open-eyed look gave him pause.

"Then why not just tell me what you're trying not to tell me!" His tone was terse and she smiled again.

"Because I promised I'd keep it quiet, but…"

"Sissy, I have no right intruding on her private life, end of subject. If you'll excuse me…" He turned to leave, but she put her hand on his arm, gaining his attention.

"Don't be an ass, Vincent," she hissed in a low whisper, knowing he was on a short fuse. "I promised Darien I wouldn't mention the call I overheard. I didn't promise I wouldn't confirm or deny the information if you asked." An eerie smile spread over her red lips, making him stay beside her. She'd gotten his attention.

"I'm losing my patience. Talk quick or I'm leaving."

She glanced around them, and only when she

was comfortable and they were secluded from prying ears did she whisper, "The poor dear did have to leave on such short notice. You know how it is sometimes—a telephone call out of the blue, a family crisis, and your whole world turns upside down." This time her eyes narrowed and he stared at her. "Good, now I have your attention." She cocked an eyebrow and Vincent knew she was right.

"Talk, Sissy..."

"You know, Vincent, at times you remind me of Lyle when we were younger. All brash and smug."

The comment hurt, and he looked at her wearily. For a second he wondered what Darien might have told her, and decided she was fishing for information. "I'll take that as a compliment. Lyle's a very accomplished man."

"Yes, mainly because he had the right woman standing beside him."

Vincent laughed out loud and she blushed slightly. It was a sight he wasn't used to and never imagined he'd see. "All right, you have my attention. Talk."

"My driver took her to the airport. It was that or she'd have had to take a later flight, and you know how hard it is to be so far away when someone you love is sick." Sissy watched several emotions wash over his face before he glared at her. His fingers gripped her upper arm and with a fake smile he turned her away from the crowd, moving toward a quiet corner.

"Who's sick, and how bad?"

"Her father. Heart related, and not fatal but serious."

"When?"

"Two days ago. Aren't you listening?" she asked in an exasperated voice.

"Why the hell didn't you call me sooner?" Vincent loomed over her, anger spilling over with his words. Again she laughed and he glared at her. She handed him her empty wine glass and pulled a small scrap of paper from her evening purse. On it was the name of the hospital and a telephone number. He looked at it and back to Sissy. "Why did you wait?"

"Because I only got through to her this afternoon. He's stable. They're doing tests, and probably an angioplasty. They have to be careful because he's diabetic."

Immediately he remembered Darien was hypoglycemic. That was part of the reason she didn't drink often. He knew she ate throughout the day in small bits to keep her sugar level. He remembered her saying it was the reverse of being a diabetic and wondered if it was hereditary. Vincent knew he'd do some fast research and learn a lot more about both in case Darien had any future problems. The thing was, she never fussed over it. Instead she quietly controlled the situation with her snacks.

It never entered his mind that it might be a problem for them, only that he needed to understand more about it to be prepared. Vincent stared at the paper in his hand for only a second before pulling his cell phone from his pocket. Sissy waited beside him, listening to him call the airport and motion for Mark to join him. She listened while he rattled off instructions. Only then did he turn to her.

"I think I've never fully appreciated you, Sissy. Thank you for this."

"Just remember. You tortured me for the information." Her conspirator's grin made him pull her to him in a bear hug.

"I'm beginning to understand Lyle a great deal more."

"Hum. It's just that I'm widely misunderstood at times." He didn't hold back his laughter and she allowed him to kiss her cheek.

"Is that what we're calling it now? I don't think I

realized the concept at first, Sissy, but I do owe you for this."

"Just go and take care of her. She needs you now, whether she wants to admit it or not." He nodded and turned away, stopping only when she put her hand on his arm. When she had his full attention, she added, "And don't screw this up again. You have no idea what it took for me to get Lyle to the auction that night. I'll be...well, never mind, but it cost me, Vincent, so don't screw up your last chance. And in case you don't realize it, it *is* your last chance with her. She's a woman with a great heart but also a determined mind. I won't be able to help you again."

****

Vincent Leighton was stunned to the point of not believing what he heard. He spun around and looked at Sissy with complete disbelief. "You set us up at the auction?"

"Of course. I knew Darien was working on the restaurant, and you mentioned a game room in your new home weeks before. When I saw the bar in the auction catalogue, I had a copy sent to you and gave Darien one myself."

He stood back and ran his hand through his hair, still not believing what he was listening to. "You?"

"Yes. I tried to get you two together for months, but either she or you kept messing up my seating arrangements with a last minute crisis. It was beginning to annoy me. I saw the bar, thought of the two of you, and figured why not?"

Vincent would have to think about all this, but later. He knew if he thought about it right now he'd most likely wring Sissy's scrawny neck. A sick chill moved through him, remembering how he'd accused Darien of engineering their meeting. On the other hand, if Sissy hadn't arranged it, he never would have met her.

"Sissy, did Darien know it was a setup?"

"Of course not, and don't you go and tell her. She'll never trust me again if you do."

"I don't know whether to kiss you or spank you, Sissy. Right about now it could go either way!"

"Yes, Lyle's familiar with the emotion!" She enjoyed his discomfort. "You know, Vincent, some men realize when they have a good thing, and they cherish it. On the outside a stranger only sees what's put out for them. It's behind closed doors where your relationship really counts. And it never ends. It changes, but there's always something lurking in the background just waiting to test you both. It's how the two of you approach those tests that makes you special to each other. It doesn't matter if other people can't see it or understand it."

Vincent took a step back and stared at her, his mind reeling from the realization she'd shared with him. He'd never given her credit for any depth beyond the surface. "Understood, Sissy. Would you like roses or orchids tomorrow?"

"Neither. I want to see you two married!"

"I'm working on it," he told her as he pulled away.

Mark was immediately at his side, listening to Vincent's instructions. If he'd looked back, he would have seen the self-satisfied grin on Sissy's face. And he would have seen the way Lyle was looking at his wife, with love and respect he'd not given either of them credit for. He'd not make the same mistake. Darien was meant for him. He'd figure out how to get her trust back.

****

During the flight he tried to sleep and couldn't. Instead, his mind was filled with Sissy's revelations. He still couldn't believe she'd engineered their meeting. Only when he thought back carefully did he remember getting the second auction catalogue. And he also remembered a brunch last spring just after he'd bought the property on Long Island. The invitations she'd extended had been numerous, and he'd turned down most of them. It annoyed him to realize he'd been engineered into position, but he was still finding it hard to be mad at Sissy. Ultimately, she'd brought him to Darien. Now he had to win her back.

****

Just after nine the next morning, he pulled up to the hospital in the Chicago suburb. He found Mr. Russell West propped in a hospital bed in a private room, Mrs. West stretched out on the bed beside him. They didn't move apart when he entered after knocking. Darien's father looked better than he'd anticipated as he moved slowly into their space.

"Mr. West, I'm sorry to intrude on your convalescence. I'm…"

"Vincent Leighton, aren't you?" asked Mrs. West.

"Yes, I am. How are you feeling?" He turned his attention back to Russell; afraid if he didn't he'd stare at Mrs. West. While she must have been shorter, she was a dead ringer for Darien, only her style was different. She wore a long, colorful skirt with a gauzy blouse over it. She had no make-up on and her hair was peppered with grey. He liked her instantly. They went through the required pleasantries before her father finally broke the tension.

"Just a small glitch; I'll be going home tomorrow. And thankfully so. This damn bed is like a rock. If I'm going to relax I want to be home in our own waterbed where we belong. The heat is great for back pain."

"Yes, so I've heard."

"You just missed Darien. She went down to the

166

office for me, a few errands that couldn't wait any longer. She'll be back but not for a few hours." Mrs. West told him.

"Oh, I'm sorry I missed her." He tried to keep his voice controlled and she smiled at him.

"I'll bet you are." She gave him a long, appraising look before her husband squeezed her hand. "You're much nicer in person than in the photograph. Although it did flatter Darien, I'm sure she was horrified. What do you want from her?"

"Patricia, let them work it out if it's to be." She turned to her husband and smiled.

"You're right, of course, but I am her mother. I'm allowed a little anger over stupidity."

"I agree with you," Vincent said, adding, "I'm studying hard..." He had to force himself not to look away, the slight hint of vulnerability he showed gave Patricia her answer.

"Good. Let me call and see if she's gotten to the office yet."

Vincent discussed the Chicago Bears with Russell, trying not to listen to Patricia's phone conversation.

"She's not there yet. Do you have a car or do you need mine?" she offered.

"I have a car downstairs, if you could give me directions," he started.

Russell stretched and yawned. His wife bent to kiss his cheek. "Rest a while and I'll walk Vincent out. Get a breath of fresh air."

"You do that. Just don't..."

"I won't. It's their life."

"Hurry back," he told her, and gave her a wink. Her lips brushed over his and held, his arm reaching to hold her. Vincent admired their open affection, realizing he and Darien were like that together. Neither of them had hesitated to show affection to the other after their Thanksgiving trip. They'd bonded as a couple and as lovers. Now he had to get her back and fix that bond, somehow strengthen it. Patricia grabbed her shoes but didn't put them on as she walked barefoot beside him down the hallway. Outside, they paused beside the main door as Vincent listened to clear directions to the food bank. He noted the cold didn't seem to affect her.

"She won't be happy to see you at first. You understand what you're walking into?"

"I think so. I deserve anything I get...except sent away."

Patricia West pulled him toward her and gave him a hug. "Don't fuck with her again, or you'll answer to me. Understand, Vincent?"

"Yes, Mrs. West. Completely." They held each other's gaze for a long moment, and it wasn't until she pulled back from the hug that she corrected him.

"Millner. I still go by Patricia Millner." She watched his reaction and shook her head. "She never told you, did she?"

****

Vincent stood dumbfounded. Millner Farm? He looked back to Patricia, staring openly at her, his mind reeling.

"I'm not surprised she didn't mention it. She'd have thought it emotional blackmail on some level. My 'husband' and I have been together thirty-three years but we've never formally married. We don't need a piece of paper to understand our commitment. But that was another time and age. I suppose for Darien, she'd want her children to be 'legitimate'."

"Don't take this the wrong way, Ms. Millner, but I'd prefer it too."

"Well, whatever works for you two. Only you can work it out."

"May I ask why you sold the property if you knew Darien loved it so much?"

"It wasn't mine to keep. It was my grandmother's home. It was sold by my mother's second husband. Darien was only eight, no, nine when my mother passed on, and her son-of-a-bitch husband sold it without letting anyone know. He could have offered it to us first, knowing it was our family home, but instead he never contacted us. It was just gone and too late to do anything about it. We were all upset. At the time Russ and I had just gotten settled here. But Darien used to spend summers there with my mother. She was born there."

"I didn't know."

"Well, we might not have been typical parents, but we loved her as best we could."

"I think you raised an amazing daughter," he told her, and meant it.

"Go on now, and give her a hug. She could use one after the last few days." She hesitated, and then decided to continue. "Vincent, Darien wasn't like most children. She didn't form attachments easily to people. Animals and plants, and us, her family. But she was always careful who she let get close. You're going to have to work to get her back. You didn't trust her, and for her, her trust was one of the best gifts she could have given you. Do you understand what I'm getting at?"

"I think so. I've had my one mistake and I won't be allowed another."

"You'll be allowed mistakes. You'll both make them, but not another one like this. If you truly love her than she has to be your first confidant, no questions asked. No matter what, you'll have to prove you'll be there for her under any circumstances."

"Before Darien, I didn't trust many women. Only my grandmother, and that's a whole different relationship."

"It's the same for Darien. If it's meant to be, then you'll find your way together." She sighed and told him it was getting late. He should head out. "Vincent, I hope it works. You two would give Russ and me beautiful grandchildren."

"Wedding first, then grandchildren!"

"You two are so modern and proper!" Patricia sauntered away with a wave of her hand, her shoes still dangling from her other hand. Vincent steered the rental according to the directions and couldn't shake the smile from his face.

****

Vincent listened to the conversation taking place just outside the office door. He'd arrived a few minutes earlier and wasn't surprised when he was recognized immediately. The middle-aged woman with frosted blonde hair and a kind voice had ushered him into the private space and told him Darien should be back any minute. He watched the shop from the doorway and couldn't help but notice the attention given to the people waiting. Everyone got a smile and personal greeting.

He glanced around the small office space, Darien looking back at him from the desk and the walls. He'd seen a few pictures she'd had framed around her apartment and two special ones she'd kept in her office. But these were different. These were proud parents' memories. From birth on, her life was documented as well as Patricia's and Russell's. The walls showed a loving family who cared deeply for each other. In every photograph that had more than one person in it; they were always touching or hugging.

Now he understood why she held back from him in the beginning, knowing if she opened herself to him it would be an emotional tie she wouldn't break easily. Vincent held up a small gold oval frame with Darien centered in it. She couldn't have been more than six, maybe seven. She was in a ballet costume and standing *en pointe*. Her dark hair was braided and wrapped around her head. There was no smile, just the determined look he'd come to know. Even then, he realized, she bit her bottom lip when in deep thought. He replaced the frame, moving to the small window across the room when he heard voices near.

****

"You had a message while you were out. It's waiting in the office for you."

"It wasn't Mom, was it?"

"No, don't panic. Just go..." Darien entered the office, but had her head turned toward the older woman, a pensive look on her face. When she turned and saw him standing there she stopped dead. Vincent watched several emotions cross her face when she saw him. He didn't wait for her to respond. He moved quickly toward her, and his arms tightened around her, swallowing her up against his body.

She let him hold her for a long time before finally pulling back. He didn't release her from his grasp, only gave her room enough to look at him. "What are you doing here?" she started, her eyes glassy, but she wouldn't let the tears come. Instead she pulled herself from his grasp, moving to the desk, using the top to rest her hands.

"I missed you, Darien," he whispered, moving closer toward her, pausing only to close the office door on his way to her side. This time he waited just a breath away. He saw the tears roll down her cheeks just before she turned to him, accepting his comfort. She didn't sob, just lost control for a few seconds before she regained it.

"How did you find out?" He laughed out loud and she smiled, knowing. "Sissy?"

"Yes, but I had to hogtie her to get the

information!"

She held his eye and they both laughed at the visual his words projected. Vincent used the pads of his thumbs to wipe away her tears. "You should have called me, Darien. I would have come with you."

Darien moved from his embrace and turned, the look on her face not believing what he said.

"Oh, yes, Vincent. I should have called you and said what? I know we're not together but I need emotional support right now? Or was I supposed to ask you to drop everything and..."

His kiss stopped her words. He'd moved closer, a hint of anger in his eyes just before he touched his lips to hers. He didn't plunder her; rather tasted her like a fine wine he'd waited to open.

When he pulled back, he simply said, "Yes, this was a crisis. You were supposed to call me and I would have dropped everything to be here for you."

"If we'd still been together, I would have." She waited only a second before adding, "You don't know how hard it was not to call you, Vincent." Darien stood to her full height and pushed her shoulders back, her eyes meeting his, refusing to blink first.

"Darien, we're just wasting time, honey. We both know we belong together and would be, if I hadn't gone completely stupid for a few days. I've apologized all I can, and I'm truly sorry for not trusting you, but keeping away from me is not going to get us straightened out."

"And what will, Vincent?"

"Spending the rest of our lives together. Being full-time partners in all that comes along, every day, good and bad, stupid or mundane. Darien, I love you. I have on some level since the first night I laid eyes on you. And it's not going to change. If you'll just take a breath and think about it, you'll admit you love me too."

"I admit it. I fell in love with you from the start, but that doesn't mean we have to act on it if it's detrimental to us both."

"I realize that, but it doesn't change the way I feel about you when I'm with you, or not. I told you weeks ago things had changed for me. You initiated the changes. One glance at the long-legged lady in green, and I knew my life was going to be different." Darien stared at him for a long time. When she didn't have any comment he pushed on. "I met your parents this morning. They're quite a couple." Her head snapped up and her eyes hardened.

"What did you tell them?"

"The truth. That I got stupid and lost you. That I still love you and want you back, permanently."

"And what did they say about it?" Hearing this, she sat on the desk chair. Vincent leaned his hip on the corner of the desk.

"We've come to terms," he started. "After all, we have your best interests at heart." She gave him her treading-on-thin-ice look and he elaborated. "Your father said it's for us to work out."

"And my mother?"

"She gave me directions here, and told me I'd used up my one chance with you. That we'd both make mistakes in our relationship through the future, but I'd had my one major error. I should keep my act together if I expected to get you back and keep you. And Darien, I want more than anything for you to be happy, but I need it to be with me. Can you understand that?" His large fingers reached to her chin, tilting her face toward him. "I won't be pushed away. Get used to me being around."

Darien laughed at his demonstrative attitude. Ultimately, she stood and dropped her arms around his neck as he pulled her between his thighs, resting her against his growing interest.

"This is what you do to me, Darien. No other

woman has had this effect on me."

"Oh, Vincent, what are we going to do?" Her head rested on his shoulder as his hands warmed her back.

"We'll work it out, I promise. We have to. I'm no good anymore without you." He heard her sigh but she didn't answer. Instead she held him tighter. "Whatever we decide is right for us. We'll figure it out together. I don't care if we're conventional or not, just as long as we decide together. You first, Darien, always, from now on. I know what we we're building and what I threw away. I'm not a stupid man. I won't do it again."

****

Their intimate moment at the food bank was cut short by the noise outside the doorway. They moved away slowly, neither wanting to break the contact.

"I'd better go see what's going on," she told him. He reached for her hand before she could leave.

"We'll go together," he told her, stopping long enough to drop his overcoat on the desk chair before following her. His suit jacket came next, minutes later, when it became apparent he could offer some help. With his sleeves rolled back, he helped pack canned goods and formula along with diapers and fresh milk. He carried cartons to waiting vehicles, pulling back from offering to drive a pregnant woman home with hers. That was when he moved from the public area and disappeared into the office. That was where Darien found him a few minutes later, his back to her, gazing out the small window.

****

"The rush is over for awhile. Thanks for helping," she told him, watching him closely. He only nodded his head but didn't turn. Inside, her stomach twisted and she knew she loved him, good and bad. It was a reality they'd both have to deal with. "It's hard to know how much we have and how little others do, sometimes. That's why my mother started the food bank. It was her way of helping without taking away what fragile pride these people have left."

"Darien, these people I met this afternoon. They all know so much about you and your family," he started.

"They're like an extended family, Vincent. Just because they don't make as much money as you or I do, or have hit hard times, doesn't make them any less precious or loveable."

"I know that," he snapped, then turned and shook his head at her, his eyes closed. "I'm sorry, I didn't mean to use that tone on you. It's just that they all seem to care about your family. I'm not used to that."

"No, you're used to being alone and blocking out anyone who tries to get close. Even me, Vincent. Even though you recognized we share more than the average couple getting together, you couldn't accept me. You used the first hint of trouble to convince yourself that I was just like everyone else, only using you."

"And I was wrong."

"Yes, but you've apologized, and I have to let it go if we're going to have a future together." His head snapped up and he stared as her lips melted into a smile.

"Do we have a future together, Darien?" She looked at him and only gave him the same small head movement she'd used at the auction. If he hadn't been staring at her he might have missed it. Instead, he let out a shout and grabbed her. When they finally pulled back from the kiss, it was to find the staff crowding the now-open doorway, all smiling and laughing.

****

"So that's where she goes when she turns down

my invitations," he was saying as Darien pulled herself back to the conversation going on around her.

"What did I miss?"

"Your mother was telling me about the volunteer hours you spend at the food bank in the city. Why didn't you tell me?" He took her hand in his across the table, not caring if her mother witnessed it.

"It didn't seem like a big deal. I've worked with them for years." Darien changed the subject effectively by signaling the waiter and asking what kind of chocolate dessert was being offered. Patricia raised an eyebrow at Vincent, but seconded Darien's choice. Vincent realized he was in love with a very complex woman, turning down the cake, but opting for a second cup of coffee. He drove them back and saw them to Russell's room. His last test seemed normal, and unless something happened, they should be able to take him home in the morning. To his relief, Darien told him she'd stay until the weekend before heading home. It would give him a few days to take care of some details he wanted to handle.

****

Darien walked him to the hospital entrance, stalling beside him, not wanting to end their time together. His arm was draped over her shoulder and she relished the feel of him next to her.

"Are you sure you don't want me to stay?" he asked, his lips pressed to her forehead.

"No, but thanks. If you stay you'll have to work over the weekend."

"Is that a hint of an invitation, Darien?" His smile would be her complete undoing.

"It could be." She didn't hold back her smile from him, knowing she'd just sealed her fate. "But no promises, all right? I'm never any good for a day or two after I travel."

"How would this sound? I'm scheduled to leave for Australia on Sunday and I'll be gone most of next week. How about we make a date for next Saturday? By then you'll be home and rested and..." His left eyebrow lifted with the rest of his question unspoken.

"Vincent, I can't. The restaurant has its grand opening that Saturday."

"I know. I got an invitation. How about I come toward the end of the evening so you can take care of business, and I'll whisk you away for a late supper, somewhere special?"

"As long as you don't tell the owners you're taking me to another restaurant to eat!"

"Deal. Darien, I'll leave you alone this weekend because I know you've had an emotional week. But, after this, you're going to have to get used to unwinding with me around." This time, his kiss let her know what he really meant. Hard pressed against her, she felt his need and her body reacted by turning soft under his. Darien spread her hands over his warm, wide back and let her hands feel his strength. She deepened the kiss when he started to pull back. Only when she ground against him did she finally stop to take note of their surroundings. Thankfully, the lobby was nearly empty and no one had witnessed their show of physical need. "Darien, I don't know if I'll make it to next Saturday..."

"We don't have a choice. I'm scheduled to come in on Saturday, and you leave on Sunday."

"I could send the plane back for you?"

"Vincent, that's sweet, but I can fly home commercial." He pulled back to stare at her and shook his head.

"All right, but I'll pick you up at the airport. We can drive home together, catch up, and say good-bye at the same time. If you're exhausted, I won't push to stay."

"I can live with that," she told him. "And you won't stay, not this week." He gave her a questioning look. "Next week will be better."

"All right, on one condition. I want something in return for the trip here."

"Always a catch," she sighed, teasing him. Vincent reached into his coat pocket and pulled out the necklace he'd had made for her at Christmas. He didn't show it to her again, simply fastened it around her neck, as she held her hair up and out of the way. When in place, her hand covered it against her throat, holding it, her tears flowing easily down her cheeks.

"Darien, don't cry, please. Wear this and you'll remember that I'm close to your heart from now on." She managed to nod, then threw her arms around him. "I can't promise I won't make mistakes in the future, Darien, but I promise they won't be unforgivable ones."

"Vincent, please don't ever hurt me like that again. I understand we're human, but I couldn't go through something like it again."

"I've never loved anyone the way I love you, Darien. I wouldn't have been as broken as I have been if I didn't. I know what I lost, and I never want to feel that way again. It hurt too much, you're right about that. Let's just agree that it was a life lesson we don't need to repeat." His brazen smile shot straight to her heart, his ego something she now understood.

"Any come to mind that you would like to repeat?" Her hand tightened on his upper arm and he knew what she was thinking. At least they were on the same track.

"Oh, Darien, we have to wait a week and a half..."

"Vincent?"

"Yes, love?" His head popped up and he looked

at her. They both burst out laughing at the same time. "What are we going to do?"

"We're going to love each other as best we can, and hope not to make too many mistakes we can't fix. I love you, Vincent Leighton, and I've never loved a man like this before."

"Thank God!" She hugged him one last time and felt him laugh into her shoulder. "Darien, do pigs have nine lives like cats?" For all of three seconds she tensed against him, and then he felt her laugh into his chest.

"I don't think so. Let's just say ours had a twin, and we'd better nurture this one a whole lot better!"

"Agreed," Vincent told her. "Go back to your family and enjoy your time with them, because when we get back to the city, I'm not going to let you go again unless I'm with you. Got it?"

"Yes. I got it. You want to be plastered by my side for all my remaining days."

"By your side, under you, over you; wherever and whenever I can."

"Deal. Now go, before I change my mind and ask you to stay."

"I will..."

"No, I'm just teasing. Go take care of business and I'll see you Saturday night."

****

Darien was relieved to see him waiting when her flight finally landed. They had had mechanical trouble and her four o'clock arrival had been pushed back. She managed to get through to Vincent on his cell and he told her he was already aware of the delay. The best part of her trip was him scooping her up in his arms and holding her tight against him. They didn't worry about her luggage. Vincent's driver took care of it. He walked her to the warmed car, pulling her tight during the drive home.

One look at her resting against his shoulder and

he knew she was beat. He also knew she didn't feel well. She'd tried to push it off to traveling but he was learning her cycle. Their only stop was for supper in Chinatown. He watched her eat ravenously after her long travel ordeal and brought her back to her apartment without question.

"Would you like coffee?" she asked, once the driver brought her bags to the apartment and receded into the night. She was leaning against the kitchen doorframe and Vincent wondered if it was holding her up.

"Nope. I'm not staying. You're exhausted and not feeling good. I'd like to stay just to hold you while you sleep, Darien, but not tonight. Next month," he whispered, leaving no option to his words. "For now I'm going; I'll call you tomorrow night." His kiss left her knees slightly more wobbly then they already were. Closing and locking the door behind him, she headed to the shower and then to bed. She didn't unpack or check her messages. Vincent had called her parents while they were waiting for supper to be served and let them know she arrived safely. Darien slept peacefully through the night and long into the next afternoon.

Chapter Thirteen

Darien smiled brightly as she introduced the owner of the new club to a realtor she'd become friendly with in the last years. The introduction had more to do with personalities than restaurants and real estate. The fifty-plus restaurateur was instantly taken with the forty-something Lenore as Darien predicted he would be. Lenore was accepting his offer of a glass of wine when she slipped away from the couple. It was after ten and she knew the grand opening had been a great success. From the end of the bar she watched as Vincent came in, smiling to the coat check girl before standing to his full height, taking in the new space.

She was surprised at the full, short, dark beard that covered his face. Anticipation ran through her. She wanted to feel the texture of it against her skin, all her skin.

Vincent's flight home had been delayed by bad weather and he was anxious to see Darien again. Each hour that ticked by seemed endless. When he'd finally reached New York, his stomach started to settle, knowing he'd be with her soon. Across the room he watched the introduction she made. He also watched how her ice green dress flowed across her body, a vision that had him hardening instantly. What struck him was the necklace she wore; his necklace, against the cleft of her throat. Her hair was up and her make-up heavy. She was a vision from his dreams and he knew tonight he'd make her his, permanently. Her facial expression changed when she saw him, moving away from the couple

181

she'd been talking with. He declined the offer of a drink from a passing waiter, reigning in his annoyance when he had to stop to talk with an old associate.

Darien watched him with a smile on her lips. She knew he was only appeasing the gentleman and hoped he was as desperate to see her as she was to see him. And to hold him.

He'd left the morning after she returned. It had been a full week with only telephone contact, each call making her miss him more. Now he was here, within her grasp. She didn't want to let go, ever. Turning her back to the crowd when her face warmed at the thoughts she'd been having, she watched him approach in the mirrors behind the bar. The large mahogany bar she'd had shipped in from Scotland. It changed the entire look and feel of the space but somehow she made it work. He watched her in the mirror too, closing the distance with each step. When he finally reached her his hand automatically went to her waist, pulling her close. Neither of them turned, rather looked at each other in the mirrors.

His hand was hot against her body, his heat radiating through her dress, his large fingers splayed against her.

"Welcome home,' she started.

"Darien, I've missed you."

She gave him a warm smile and was favored with one of his mischievous ones in return. "The restaurant is wonderful. You did a great job."

"Thank you, Vincent. Considering..." She laughed as he surveyed the bar they both leaned against.

"Interesting. Mahogany?"

"Yes, don't gloat. It's not attractive," she told him. "Although I could get used to the new you. Did you grow this for me?" His smile told her he did.

"You look beautiful tonight. I wish I'd gotten here earlier. I don't like to think about all the men who have studied you tonight." He accepted a drink from the bartender and nodded his thanks.

"I didn't notice anyone tonight. I've been watching the door for you." She turned to watch the smile that spread across his lips, lips her hand reached up to touch. It was brief, just her index finger running along his bottom lip as the rest of her fingers stroked his newly-covered chin. The texture was warm and soft even after a week. Darien watched the visible chill run through him, biting her bottom lip to hold back her smile.

"Not fair," he started, getting lost in the green eyes sparkling back at him. "How long before you can make a graceful exit?"

She surveyed the dwindling crowd and decided she'd had enough. "Now, if you're ready..." A man's arm came across her shoulders and both she and Vincent straightened. "Vincent Leighton, this is Allan Cross, proud owner of this new establishment. Allan this is Vincent." The two men eyed each other until he took his arm off Darien, and then Vincent reached to shake his other outstretched hand.

"An amazing space," Vincent said.

"All thanks to Darien. She's quite a treasure."

"Yes, I know." The intense stare between the two men continued until Darien laughed at them both.

"Relax, boys," she joked. "Allan, don't tease him. Vincent, he's just busting your chops because you got his original bar. Allan is a man who adores blondes, just like Lenore, who I just introduced him to." All three of them glanced to the woman a few feet away, Darien calling her closer to introduce her to Vincent. When egos had settled she told Allan she was leaving. At the door he made a great show of kissing her on both cheeks, holding her in a bear hug a little longer than necessary. She was laughing by the time they reached the car, and Vincent was on edge. Only after being safely ensconced in the back of the private vehicle did she turn, taking Vincent's face between her hands, guiding him to her lips.

"I've missed you more than I wanted to."

"Darien, you have no idea…" Their second kiss lasted through most of their drive. When the car stopped she realized they were at the blues club he'd taken her to the night after the auction. "I promised you a special supper…" he told her with a look in his eyes that didn't convey food, only hunger.

"I'm starved, Vincent."

He reached for her hand to help her from the vehicle. "Come with me, Darien." She did, willingly, with great hope in her heart. The club was crowded but Vincent managed to get them a quiet back booth. They enjoyed the meal while catching up on the time they'd been apart during his meetings last week and the weeks in December. It was then that he finally thanked her for his presents. He wondered aloud how she knew about Betty Page. She only gave him an elusive smile.

"What made you grow the beard this week?" she asked, not resisting the urge to let her fingers comb through it again. He held her close to his growing interest while they danced.

"An act of rebellion for having to leave you." Darien liked his answer, and told him so with a kiss. She felt bold in the surroundings, their situation limiting the contact she wanted to pursue.

"Will you come with me tomorrow morning, Darien? There's something I want to show you."

"Where to?"

"Trust me?" Her eyes flashed with gold trim once more and he burst out laughing. "I love it when you look at me like that. It says so much." When the song changed, he guided her back to their table just as their coffee was being poured. This time his hand reached her thigh under the table, making her straighten.

"Where are you taking me tomorrow?" Her voice faltered when his finger traced from her thigh to knee. With each pass she melted slightly. Darien realized two could play, especially since the banquet had a long white tablecloth to block them from prying eyes. She moved closer toward him, his arm raised along the back of the seat. Darien tucked herself against him. Her hand lazily dropped to his lap, her thumbnail glossing over his endowment. He'd been semi-erect when she moved closer. Now he steeled under her touch.

"Darien, is this how our lives are going to be?" He glanced down only slightly. She watched him pick up his cup and make a show of bringing it to his lips, his eyes surveying the crowded dance floor before them.

"Will it drive you crazy, Vincent?" Her words were a whisper against his ear. He shuddered when she spoke and she felt him surge in her palm. "Oh, Vincent, we are going to have fun, aren't we?"

"Yes, Darien. We are." He signaled for the check and she pulled away, knowing if she didn't, she'd take their teasing a step further. He nodded his understanding of her pulling back, watching as she gathered her purse, when they both saw the shadow near. A dread weight came over them.

The granite glare on Vincent's face made her look across the table. Mike Guran stood across from them, a strange look on his face.

Darien instantly went taut when she recognized him, and finally understood what had happened. She knew immediately who had told Vincent she'd been with Mark at his apartment. It was all so stupid, the time they spent apart because of this man, this man who now stared at her like she was a slab of meat on a market table, waiting to be bought. Her hands fisted at her sides and she looked back to Vincent.

"Can we leave now, Vincent?"

"Yes, this place has lost its appeal." He reached to her, ignoring the man watching them. She slid along the booth to take his hand, rising very close beside him. They turned to walk away without comment, and would have if Mike Guran hadn't grabbed at her shoulder. She stopped and turned to the vicious man with beady eyes, and the club around her disappeared. Darien only saw an adversary and didn't care if she made a spectacle of herself or not.

"Don't ever touch me," she hissed at him. Vincent pulled her to his side and stepped forward. "Don't bother, Vincent. He's not worth the effort."

Vincent looked to Darien and back to Mike.

"Vincent, I see you've gone back to slumming again. Or was she just training your apprentice for you?" It was obvious the man had had too much to drink. The club manager was beside them instantly.

"Mr. Leighton, Ms. West, I hope you enjoyed your meal tonight. Is there anything I can do for you?" The wise man watched Vincent for a clue as to the encounter that was about to take place in the center of his club. He watched Vincent size up Mike Guran once more and glance back to Darien. His arm was around her waist and she had her arm locked behind his back. For one intense moment nobody was sure what would happen. Finally Vincent spoke.

"Just take out the garbage...," he said, all three of them laughing openly. All except for Mike. He glared at them until they turned to leave, then he again grabbed for Darien's arm.

****

She reacted before thinking the situation through. As if in slow motion, the club manager and

Vincent, as well as Mike, watched her pull from Vincent's body. In one step her knee connected squarely with Mike's precious equipment. She didn't hold back and used her full body weight to make contact. His face went blank just before the air rushed out of his lungs in a loud whoosh. They watched him start to crumple to the floor while the manager snapped his fingers and nodded to a waiter to catch the collapsing man before he hit. When his body was stable, his face cherry red, she finally spoke.

"That's the second time you've accosted me, Mr. Guran. Touch me again, ever, and I'll file charges against you." She held his eye and he glanced away. A tense moment passed with most of the crowd around them completely unaware. Darien turned back to Vincent, loving him more for the smile he gave her. "Vincent, please take me home," she said.

The club manager walked them toward the front door, apologizing for the inconvenience, promising them he'd make sure they weren't bothered in the future if they chose to come back. Darien assured him that she was becoming quite at home in the space and she'd talk Vincent into another meal in the near future. At the door he followed them outside, the difference in light and sound almost deafening them by comparison.

"Ms. West, may I take this opportunity to thank you for doing what myself and several other patrons have wanted to do for a very long time." He gave her a light kiss on each cheek before moving to shake Vincent's hand. "I assure you, Mr. Leighton: Ms. West will be carefully looked after when ever she graces my establishment.

"Let's just go back to Vincent and Darien, and I'll assume she's in good company if she's here on her own."

"Absolutely." He paused and smiled at them. "A

rare woman indeed, Vincent." He spun away, moving back into the dark club, leaving Darien and Vincent alone. His car pulled up and only after they were seated and moving did she dare to speak.

"Are you pissed?"

"Not at you, Darien. I'm quite proud of how you handled yourself. I'm thinking I'm a little disappointed that you didn't need me to be your white knight and ride to your rescue."

"I can think of much better things for you to do for me...and to me... than take care of a jerk like him."

"I can think of a great many, but most of them start with getting you out of this dress."

"I like your train of thought. Tell me more," she whispered, moving closer toward him.

"I'll tell you about it upstairs..." His hand angled her chin toward her lips. He hit the intercom button, telling the driver to take them through the park as he drew her across his lap, taking the kiss he'd waited weeks for. With her arm around his neck and her lips to his, Vincent let his hands roam along her body, feeling what he'd missed for so long. When they'd built up to a fevered pitch they realized the car was slowing in front of his building.

Darien managed to scramble off his lap and pull her cape around her, but she couldn't hide her ravished lips, full and red from his attentions, or her nipples budded into tight raspberries pushing against two layers of material, wanting more attention. Only they would know how he'd used the ride to tease her into a sexual fury. Each pin had been pulled from her hair and tossed onto the car floor. Only her decorative combs had been stashed in his jacket pocket. His fingers had run along her scalp and feathered the long waves of her hair back around her shoulders.

****

In the bright light of the building lobby, Vincent was welcomed home by the doorman who smiled shyly at Darien. Their small talk while waiting for the elevator was just ending when the bell announcing the arrival of the cab was drowned out. The front doors were flung open, glass slamming back into place. All three of them turned in unison to see Mike Guran stagger into the lobby. His loud words were slurred. Darien easily took a step behind Vincent.

"Don't even think about it, Mike...," Vincent started, but he had already set his weight in a defensive stance. The doorman watched in quiet confusion and ultimate horror as the drunken resident plowed toward the other couple. They all managed to interpret a curse word here or there from the ramblings spilling from his mouth. Obviously Vincent and Darien knew why he was so angry. The doorman was just an innocent witness to the man's drunken rage.

"Amazon slut," he managed to spew toward them, and Vincent drew a deep breath. He pulled his overcoat off and dropped it into Darien's arms. Next came his suit jacket.

"Vincent, he's not worth the effort."

"I know, Darien, but I'll feel so much better." She laughed aloud and took a second step back.

"Should I call the police, Mr. Leighton?" the doorman asked.

"No, they're busy enough." They watched Mike come forth with another round of vicious talk aimed at Darien and himself. It was the last straw. Vincent simply took one step forward, his fist finding its pudgy target easily. One satisfying punch to the man's stomach, and a second to his jaw, had him sprawled on the marble lobby floor. Vincent shook his fist a few times before leaning down and hauling the man back to his feet by the front of his shirt. He waited for Mike's vision to focus on him before he spoke.

"Don't ever go near my future wife again. Anywhere, do you understand me, Mr. Guran? Whether on the street or in a restaurant or especially in this building, don't ever dare look or speak to her again, let alone try to touch her." Vincent's eyes glazed black and Mike seemed to be out of his earlier drunken state. "This was a warning tonight. Go near my wife under any circumstances and I'll make sure you're physically unable to harass any woman, ever again." He dropped the front of Mike's shirt and watched him crumple to the floor a second time. "I think he might need some air," Vincent started to say as the doorman dragged him toward the entry.

Darien watched him carefully, turning back to the waiting elevator. For the entire ride up neither said a word. Only after they were safely locked away in Vincent's apartment did she turn to him, after dropping his coat and jacket on the hall table. She slipped off her cape, laying it beside his.

"I'll get some ice for your hand...," she told him, slipping away. Vincent tugged his tie off and dropped it on the back of the sofa. He rolled back his sleeves and stood at the balcony door waiting for her return.

****

Darien didn't stifle the gasp that came from deep within her as she entered the living room and realized it was still decorated. All the lights were on and she stood in the center of the room turning in a slow circle, her hand still holding the dish towel with chips of ice folded inside.

"I never thought it would still be decorated."

"I couldn't bear to take it down, not until I'd had a chance to kiss you next to the tree and under the mistletoe."

Darien turned back to him, realizing she was still holding the ice pack. "Here," she started as she moved closer, reaching for his hand and applying the iced towel to his knuckles. She leaned up on her toes and kissed his lips. "The tree has to come down, Vincent. It's a fire hazard."

"I know. My housekeeper has been telling me the same thing for weeks. But you see; I needed to see you beside the tree, just once. I needed to be able to carry the image with me for the rest of my days."

"I'll help you pack it up tomorrow."

"Tomorrow evening. In the morning you promised to come with me."

"You never told me where," she reminded him, carefully touching a branch and watching the dried needles rain down onto the carpet.

"I know. It's a surprise." Vincent studied her for a long time, standing in front of the tree, and knew he'd never love any other woman the way he loved her, with all his heart and soul.

Darien watched him watching her and blushed under his watchful eye. She wasn't sure what to expect, but Vincent asking her to put up a pot of coffee wasn't it. He excused himself while she did and came back to meet her in the kitchen, his dark suit exchanged for soft jeans and a heavy sweater.

He handed her two insulated stainless-steel travel mugs to fill and knew he was confusing her. "Are you ready?"

"I'm not sure. Suddenly I feel overdressed."

"Not for long. Next stop your apartment for you to change." There were no long discussions. She accepted her cape when he dropped it over her shoulders and watched him swap his long overcoat for a short shearling jacket before they left the apartment. His truck was waiting beside the building entrance and the doorman assured them that Mr. Guran had had some fresh air and was safely upstairs in his own apartment under the watchful eye of his older sister. The drive across town to her building had Darien laughing.

"He lives with his spinster sister?" Vincent mumbled, enjoying the irony.

"I suppose she holds the purse strings too," Darien added. "No wonder he's such an unhappy man."

"He's not our problem." Parked a few doors away from her townhouse, Vincent made it quite clear they weren't going to get comfortable. Once inside, he asked Darien to change into warm clothes.

She took her cue from him, changing quickly even though she was a little confused. She'd been imagining a long night in bed and instead he wanted to go for a drive? Not until they were back in his truck did she finally ask. "I got the impression you wanted to take me out of that green dress, Vincent. What changed tonight?"

"A lot, Darien. And I will take you out of that dress in the near future. I just felt this was important to handle first."

****

There was no need to ask where he was driving her at four-thirty in the morning. As soon as she saw the entrance to the Midtown tunnel she knew their destination. The road was almost empty during their drive. When he left the expressway, he stopped in a service center to get them fresh coffee.

Nearing five-thirty in the morning he pulled into the driveway of the Millner farm, parking the truck near where the front of the house would one day stand. Darien stared out the windshield and couldn't speak, afraid she'd say the wrong thing. The both sat quiet for a long time, sipping their coffee and watching the sun rise over the land.

"It's magnificent. Now I understand why you moved the bedrooms to the other side of the house.

Morning sun..."

"Yes, it seemed right."

"Darien, why didn't you tell me about the house, about it being your grandmother's land, about you being born here? I don't understand."

"It seemed like a low card to pull. You owned it fair and square. It's not like you cheated me out of it in a card game."

"But it would have explained so much."

"But technically none of it mattered at the time. You were a polite stranger who wound up owning something I was attached to. And if you remember, I was trying very hard to keep my distance from you."

"That didn't work so well, did it?" His laughter brightened her smile and she resolved to admit he'd annoyed her from the start. "I'd like to get a few things clarified, Darien. It's important."

"All right," she said, turning toward him.

"If your father hadn't gotten sick I never would have realized the significance if the property. I never would guess the M as your middle initial stood for Millner. A detail that my research on you didn't turn up."

"I know."

"Did you know we were set up?" The look on Darien's face answered all his remaining questions. She'd been as oblivious as he.

"What are you talking about? I thought we had this conversation. Do you still think I went out of my way to insinuate myself into your life?" His kissing her was the only way to curb her growing hostility, which was starting to surface. She started to pull away but he held her shoulders tight. When he pulled back to look, she glared at his hands on her shoulders.

"Darien, it was Sissy. She set us both up. I'm sorry I accused you. I only found out at the museum dedication when she told me your father was ill."

She pulled back from him, studying his face with a quizzical look.

"Sissy? How?" As soon as she said the words her eyes closed. "The bar!"

Vincent let himself relax back into his seat. "Yes, and apparently she owes Lyle big time for it, although I don't want to know just what 'it' is exactly! Darien, she claims she'd been trying to get us together for months."

"Poor Sissy. I kept declining her invitations. If only I'd known you were waiting for me."

"What would you have done?"

She laughed openly. "Probably exactly the same thing I did when we finally met. Run as far away as I could."

"Why? Tell me why."

"Because a man like you is dangerous to women. You make us think we can't survive without you by our side."

"Would it be so bad to have me beside you?"

"Yes and no, Vincent. You're a double-edged sword."

"Darien, look at me." She turned to him and he kissed her lightly on the lips. "Come with me," he finished, just before opening the truck door, letting in the early morning cold.

****

Darien looked at Vincent as if he'd gone crazy, pulled her collar closer to her throat, and followed him. They wandered hand in hand through the dew-moistened grass around the old foundation. The sun was just breaking through the layer of night sky when he stopped, pulling her to him.

"Darien, I love you. It would make me very happy if you'd marry me and spend the rest of your life with me, here and in the city." He waited a beat for a response but then pushed on before she could speak. "We could turn this into our weekend home for a few years and then maybe eventually move out here permanently. Whatever we decide, we both need to be in the city several days a week for business. This could be our getaway. And with a little luck you might even give birth to our children here."

****

Darien was dumbfounded by his words. So much swam through her mind. None of it made sense. He watched her face for a sign and finally started to laugh. "It's not a death sentence, Darien. I'm asking you to be my wife, my partner in this life, and possibly throw in a few kids if you'd like."

"Vincent, I drive you crazy, and you confound me at most turns. We'd be..."

"Never dull, that's for sure. Darien, I don't want to change you. I like the feisty woman who turned me down originally. I fell in love with the buxom broad who laughs easily and loves hard. And I want to love you until I die because you're the woman I've waited all my life for." He hesitated but continued, uncomfortable with verbalizing his feelings. "I have only one request and it's a big one. Nonnegotiable." Vincent watched Darien brace for his words.

"Go ahead," she managed to say.

"I like your parents. I truly do, and with time they'll come to accept me. I think they raised an amazing daughter but..."

"But, go ahead, Vincent. Be honest. What is it?"

"I want our children to be legitimate. I want that stupid piece of paper that doesn't mean anything in the long run except what we allow it to stand for. But I want it anyway. Who knew I'd turn out to be so conventional? What about you? What do you want?"

"I want you as my husband, Vincent. My life hasn't been the same since the night of the auction. And I want something else from you, a promise you won't break."

"I'll always give you my trust, Darien. I've learned my lesson."

"I know that, but I want you to promise I can give birth in a hospital if I want to." Darien watched him visibly relax; she knew she'd made the right decision.

"Yes to the hospital if that's your choice, as long as it's yes to being my wife?"

"Yes, Vincent. But you know it won't be easy."

"Nothing worthwhile usually is, but we'll be together and that will see us through. I love you, Darien. Marry me?"

"I love you too, Vincent. Yes, I'll marry you, if you truly understand I'm not doing it just to get my hands on your land or your home." She started out teasing, then sobered at her own words. He grabbed both her hands and pulled her close.

"I'm sorry I said that; I was angry. I know you'd rather never see this place again if you thought I really believed it. I'll sell this and you can pick any place you want if it would make you feel better. I want a home with you, Darien, here or anywhere you choose."

"And you'll always be responsible for Thanksgiving dinners?" She pulled her bottom lip between her teeth to hold back a smile.

"I wasn't sure if you remembered that, but yes. Thanksgiving is not your responsibility. All the others are though...," he teased as he leaned down to suck her bottom lip between his. Her hands slid along his chest and behind his head, drawing him tighter. His need pressed against her, heating her own arousal.

"Oh, Vincent..." Darien left him abruptly. Just as he was going to follow her she returned with the car blanket, tossing it to the ground in the area where the master bedroom would eventually be built, lowering herself onto it. She reached a hand to him in invitation.

Vincent grabbed her hand as his lifeline, slowly lowering beside her. They struggled with coats and sweaters, boots and jeans and neither of them cared or stopped until he was buried deep inside her, moving over her with a smooth rhythm that built inside them both until she called out his name into the morning light, taking him with her down the chasm he'd built inside them both. When he was able to move it was only to shift his weight from her. She felt his tugging at his jeans and pinched his firm buttocks under her fingers.

"Don't go yet," she managed.

"I'm not," he told her as he dropped back. Only after an exquisite kiss did he pull back and reach for her hand. Vincent slipped the complimenting ring on her finger and knew he'd come home.

****

Only hours later, when they slowly wandered into a diner for lunch, sated and happy, did she really study the engagement ring he'd slipped on her finger.

"It's beautiful, Vincent. Thank you for wanting me for your wife."

"You're beautiful, and you deserve much more. Give me this lifetime, Darien. I promise to get you everything I humanly can."

"Can you love me honestly and openly every day?"

"I can only tell you I'll do my best. And you're an amazing incentive package!"

"I can buy my own jewels, Vincent. I don't need lots of sparkly jewelry to reinforce your love. Your kiss and your touch will tell me every day. That's what I want from you, what I'll expect."

Dragging her left hand to his lips, he kissed it lightly before looking over the top of the menu, waiting while the blush from her cheeks subsided. "Darien, I will buy you lots of jewels, but they'll all come with my love." He held her eye and she gave him her auction house nod. "Now, I'm starving. What are we going to eat?"

****

Their drive back to the city in the early afternoon was uneventful but informative. Vincent asked Darien what her schedule was like the next day. After giving him a brief description, she turned in her seat, letting her hand drift to his neck, her fingers teasing his chin through the layer of hair she was becoming so attached to.

"Want me to cancel it all so we can stay home in bed?" He gave her a sidelong glance with a smile.

"Yes, but save it for a day we can both call in sick. Stay with me tonight, all night?"

"Yes, if I can have two wishes," she teased.

"Go ahead. What's the price I have to pay to keep you in my bed all night?"

"It's going to be steep. Think you can handle it?"

"I'll do my best. Try me."

"First I want to stop home and get a change of clothes."

"Done, no problem. We can bring over anything and everything you want. The back of the truck is empty, with lots of room. Second?" They were nearing the tunnel entrance when she finally spoke.

"You have to promise to let me start taking down the living room displays."

"With one exception,"

"What?" He gave her a second glance, the light in the tunnel slicing across her wind-burned cheeks.

"First, nothing gets touched until we get a chance to make love on the floor under the tree. Second, my statue doesn't get packed away. She stays out year round."

"Fine, until we start a family. Then she goes in

your study."

"Deal." His hand reached across the console and held hers lightly as he directed the truck toward Darien's apartment.

****

He tried to get her to bring more personal items to his place, but she was adamant that this would get her through the night and tomorrow. She'd have to come back to her office in the afternoon and could pick up anything she might need.

Darien knew he wasn't happy, but she also knew she couldn't just move into his place overnight. They made love on the floor under the tree several times before drifting off to sleep. She'd woken to a darkened sky with him beside her, his arm holding her.

"Don't go, I'm too comfortable," he told her as he stretched beside her.

"I'm hungry and cold. You can fix the cold part but you have to feed me soon."

"Such demands already. I don't know…" She watched as he moved easily to his feet, reaching a hand down to help her up. "Food first or shower?"

"Quick shower, then food," she decided. Their shower wasn't anything resembling quick, but they both reveled in the feelings they stirred within each other. She'd pulled on a pair of leggings and a long tee-shirt sans bra, and found it hard not to run her hand along his taut, bare belly as they worked in the kitchen side by side. He fed her slices of apple and cheddar cheese while marinating the chicken and she cleaned lettuce for their salad. Their movements were precise in the space and conversation was easy.

****

"What kind of wedding would you like?"

Darien thought before she answered and told him the truth. "A year ago I would have said a big circus with hundreds of guests and all the trimmings. Right now, all I want is for us to be married. The show doesn't seem so important any more. I'd say family and a few close friends."

"How long of an engagement do you want to pull it all together?"

"I thought an engagement was supposed to be the time when we make sure we're right for each other, and planning the wedding is a test. If we survive as a couple long enough to get through the preparations, we stand a shot at the future."

Vincent wiped his hands on a towel and tossed it aside. He moved behind her, his hands cupping her breasts as his lips found the back of her neck. "We know we're right, and wasting time isn't going to change that." His fingers were doing wonderful things to her. She warmed all the way to her toes, her head dropping back against his shoulder, the salad long forgotten to his touch.

"Want to go to Las Vegas? We could elope." Darien dropped the knife from her hand, turning in his arms, taking his mouth to hers as she ground against his enthusiasm.

"Your mother would kill me if I took you to Vegas. Three months, Darien. Can you pull something together in a few weeks? How does the beginning of April sound? Wherever and whatever you decide, I'll go along with, except a long engagement." She pulled back and stared openly at him. "What?" He reached past her, grabbing a handful of sliced carrots, slipping one between her lips before tasting one himself.

"The auction was the second Tuesday in October, right?"

"Yes. Don't say you want to wait until October, Darien?" She smiled and kissed his cheek.

"How does the second Tuesday in March sound? Six months from the night we finally met?"

"You mean six months from the time Sissy

finally maneuvered us together?"

"I think I'll ask her to be my matron of honor. Can you handle that?"

"She'll be thrilled, Darien. Yes, and if you can put together a wedding that will satisfy the little girl inside you in that amount of time, I'm all for it."

"Second Tuesday in March it is."

"Settled. Now, until then, are you going to live here with me or not?" He moved away and turned the chicken on the grill. It sizzled and spit and smelled wonderful.

"I don't know, but now that you mentioned it, I assume you want to live here when we're in the city?"

"That's one possibility." They set out the food and ate ravenously at the small counter in the kitchen. "We could stay here, you could go wild with color and texture or..."

"Or what?"

"Or we could find another place we both like or maybe..."

"Vincent?" She put down her fork and stared at him.

"I don't like the idea of you being in this building with Guran. I've thought about several ways of getting him out of the building, but I don't want to give him the satisfaction of knowing I hate him so. And I don't want to put you in any more situations where he can confront you, drunk or not."

"But you told me you loved this place and the view. Don't let somebody like Guran ruin it for us."

"What about your townhouse, Darien? Your studio is on the ground level and there are the other two apartments above yours."

"That has possibilities, but I'm sure the other tenants would like a say in the matter."

"Actually, that's not as much of a problem as you might think. Don't decide now. Think about it. We can renovate your place or find another apartment."

"I do like my neighborhood. Could you handle several flights of stairs every day?"

"It would keep us both in shape, but you'll work an elevator into the design for my aging days. Besides, I have fond memories of long good-byes at that elevator door." He winked and she blushed.

"Oh, I will, huh? You've got this all thought out. You won't have the view," she added.

"No, but we'll have a home together. That's what counts."

"There's a wonderful elementary school just two blocks away."

"I know. I've spent some time in the neighborhood in the last weeks."

"Really?" Her facial expression said more than her one-word answer.

"I wanted to be sure of what I was buying before I bought it," he told her. Darien stared in complete disbelief.

"What are you saying? You bought my building?"

"Yes, last month."

"Were you planning on throwing me out if I didn't accept your engagement ring?" Something snapped inside her. She was up scraping her dish into the disposal. He shook his head at her and left the room, which only made her more furious.

When he returned, she'd cleared the counter and was scrubbing at something in the sink. Whatever it was, he was glad it wasn't him. Vincent pulled back his smile and moved behind her, unfolding the paper he held open for her to see.

She started to push it aside when her name caught her eye. Only then did she give the document her full attention. "I don't understand."

"I said I bought the building and I did. I just didn't add that I'd gifted it to you."

"Vincent, even you can't give me a building." He pulled her hands from the sink, drying them with a towel before handing her the document. She read it carefully and looked at him. "Apparently you can...but this is dated, Vincent. We'd broken up when you did this." Green eyes rimmed with gold stared at him.

"Yes. Either way you were destined to own the building, married to me or not."

"You bought me my studio and apartment, even though we were broken up?"

"I wanted you to always have a home, no matter what. And I knew you'd never accept the deed to the Glen Cove property. And before you ask, the other tenants are aware of the sale and have been given notice."

"What if I decided not to marry you? Then what?"

"Then you could rewrite their leases as you liked."

"Vincent Leighton, you amaze me."

"Darien, that's how I feel all the time now, amazed by you and how you make my life so much happier and filled with love." She turned in his arms and let him hold her tight. "Hell, I even like myself more since I met you. I look at life differently, Darien, and that's your influence."

"The renovation will take ages," she started. "I see the whole place in shades of tan..." Even she couldn't hold back her laughter.

"You've added color to my life, Darien. You can't back down now. No, I think you'll design us a home with attitude."

"What attitude?"

"Ours, toward life. Bright and hopeful. Like our future together."

She didn't manage to say anything with words. Instead she buried her head against his shoulder, giving him her auction nod. "Want to stay here or move to something temporary during the renovation?"

"Let's stay here until our home is ready. And, Vincent, I can handle Guran. Don't ever worry about him, please. He's not worth you getting an ulcer."

"All right, as long as you promise never to get on the elevator with him, even if you're not alone."

"I promise. Vincent, he was the one who called you, isn't he?"

"Yes."

"Then we'll not give him the satisfaction of leaving. We'll both live here until we're married and the townhouse is renovated."

"Whatever will keep my wife happy," he told her as his head dropped toward hers.

"Take me to bed, Vincent, make me happy there." He scooped her up in his arms and carried her back to the living room.

"This is probably going to be our first and last Christmas in this apartment. Let's enjoy the scenery a while longer." Darien kneeled beside him, slipping her hands under the waistband of his sweatpants. Her nails dragged lightly along his thighs as she pulled them from his hips, baring him to her. Her cheek rested against him and she sighed.

"Vincent?" His hands ran through her hair as her breath caressed him.

"Darien?"

"Just think of the possibilities…" Her words were a mere whisper against his skin, her green eyes glancing up to see the smile spread across his lips.

"I know, Darien, I know. And the best part, besides that you actually fell in love with me, is…"

"Is that we're both tall!" She engulfed him with her lips, pulling him into the warmth of her mouth, showing him how much she did love him.

About the Author...

Having been born and raised on Long Island, NY, my husband and I were both eager to leave the urban lifestyle behind us and explore our futures. With his encouragement I'm living my dream of writing romance novels full time. Our new rural setting allows us time to enjoy each other and leaves me guiltless hours in my imagination indulging my other passion.

Visit Cheryl at www.cornellromance.com

Other Champagne titles you might enjoy:

HOW MUCH YOU WANT TO BET? by Melissa Blue – Neil never thought a game of pool could change the course of her life, but when she plays against Gibland Winifred the Third she knows she's liable to lose both the game and her heart.

CATASTROPHE by Sharon Buchbinder – CATS! Twenty-three of them! They and their owner are being evicted, and their handsome neighbor doesn't want to lose any of them, especially the curly-haired, curvaceous woman. Can they come up with a rescue plan?

HIBISCUS BAY by Debby Allen – Picture love on a sun-drenched white sand beach surrounded by hibiscus-covered cliffs, with your yacht anchored in a blue Mediterranean Sea.

TASMANIAN RAINBOW by Pinkie Paranya – A concert violinist grapples with remote ranch life, intrigue and the mystery of a missing diary, the peril of a flood in which all could be lost, and the undeniable attraction of the man who would do anything to protect his son.

THREE'S THE CHARM by Ellen Dye – Rachel vowed never to speak to her ex-husband again. But her beloved horse falls ill and Heath is the only vet within three counties of West Virginia mountains, and some vows need to be broken.

THE CHRISTMAS CURSE by Marianne Arkins – Dressed as Mrs. Claus, Molly meets the man of her dreams, who turns out to be a nightmare, in a broken-down elevator. Her Christmas Curse is right on track.

www.ingramcontent.com/pod-product-compliance
Lightning Source LLC
Chambersburg PA
CBHW072054170626
46813CB00004B/1342